SAFE HARBOUR

Working as a hostess on a cruise ship, Beth Walker meets Ryan Donovan, and is drawn to his soft Irish lilt and mischievous eyes. It's love at first sight, each swept away by the other like the waves on the sea. But when Beth learns of a dark secret Ryan's been harbouring, she feels her only choice is to break it off and never see him again. Despite the misery it causes them, it looks like her plan will work — until she discovers she is carrying Ryan's child . . .

NATALIE KLEINMAN

SAFE HARBOUR

Complete and Unabridged

LINFORD
Leicester

First published in Great Britain in 2014

First Linford Edition
published 2016

A catalogue record for this book is available
from the British Library.

ISBN 978–1–4448–2766–8

Published by
F. A. Thorpe (Publishing)
Anstey, Leicestershire

Set by Words & Graphics Ltd.
Anstey, Leicestershire
Printed and bound in Great Britain by
T. J. International Ltd., Padstow, Cornwall

This book is printed on acid-free paper

1

Gazing out into the harbour, Beth took a deep shuddering breath and allowed the misery she still felt about Gerry to flood over her. *How could I have been taken in for so long?* she wondered, looking at a nearby seal, its mournful eyes apparently in sympathy with her.

'At least give me a chance to explain,' he'd said. What was to explain? He was married, for heaven's sake.

Mostly she was doing okay now, but every so often she had to acknowledge how badly hurt she'd been. An innate honesty forced her to admit to a certain amount of relief. After all, things hadn't been going all that well for a long time, but the blow when it came had still been a shock. This temporary work had come at just the right time.

She pulled out her phone and texted Claire. 'Sorry about the chicken pox but thanks for the job. Wishing you less spotty.'

Beth looked out over the water, taking in the atmosphere. The seemingly removed background noises of the quayside activity mingled with the unmistakable sound of other vessels straining at their hawsers like horses in their starting blocks, anxious to be off, as if they couldn't wait to do what they were made for and head out to sea. Beth was lost in thought until a loud intermittent beeping had her reaching for her mobile again. She turned her back to the rail, leaning on it while she read Claire's reply: 'Spotty? There's only the one. They're all joined up!'

Laughing, Beth looked up to see what was possibly the handsomest man she'd ever encountered coming straight towards her.

He was moving with unconscious ease, a gentle breeze ruffling his curls. They were very dark brown with just a hint of red and were glinting in the sunlight that had peeped out sometime during the afternoon. The naval backdrop didn't do him any harm either. All thoughts of Gerry disappeared as she assimilated the advancing vision. *Oh My God, he's gorgeous! What wouldn't I give?* She hoped he couldn't read her mind! Even at this distance she could see the fun twinkling in his eyes hinting at a playfulness he was making little effort to disguise. Long legs and graceful hips supported a body that was no stranger to the gym. In spite of the fact that experience should have taught her the dangers of falling too hard and too fast, she felt herself drawn to this man before they were even introduced, wondering if maybe she'd left Gerry further behind than she'd thought. She fired off another quick text before he reached her.

'Adonis spotted. Talk later.'

Adonis wasn't alone. He was pushing a wheelchair carrying a lovely young girl who looked up at him as they neared Beth and said: 'You'll have to bend down if you want me to hear you.

You're nearly in the clouds up there.'

Solid-looking and standing at least six inches taller than Mr Average, this giant of a man was the epitome of tall, dark and handsome — a walking cliché if ever she saw one. He looked down at her, an eyebrow raised provocatively, just as her phone demanded her attention again. She ignored it.

'Sure it's a beautiful afternoon, isn't it? Far too good to waste unpacking. I'm Ryan, and this,' he said, smiling down at the girl 'is Siobhán.' He put a hand on the girl's shoulder and there was no doubting the protection in the gesture. Beth was astonished to see such gentleness in a man of his size.

The soft lilt of his voice curled around every nerve ending and she found herself wondering what had happened to the young woman with the broken heart.

'Beth; Beth Walker.'

'Hello, Beth. And is this your first cruise?'

'Yes, it is; well, no, it isn't, not really.'

4

His eyes crinkled with amusement. 'Both. Sure isn't that just wonderful.'

'Stop laughing at her, Ryan,' said Siobhán, though she was smiling herself.

Beth threw her a grateful look. 'I mean, yes, it's my first time on a cruise ship, and no it isn't my first cruise as such because I'm a member of staff.'

'Are you now? Cabin stewardess? Waitress?' He raised his eyebrow again in a question.

I bet he has no idea how gorgeous he looks when he does that. Beth took in his muscle-bound torso, the shadow on his chin where he was beginning to need a shave, the slight imperfection of his mouth that only accentuated his attractiveness.

'Neither,' she said, pulling herself together and allowing her professional smile to settle onto her face. 'I'm your hostess; my job is to make the trip as pleasurable as possible. I'll be meeting you officially at this evening's cocktail party.'

'We'll look forward to it, won't we, Siobhán?' He turned his head to look at the harbour. 'I may be wrong, but aren't we moving?'

He wasn't wrong. The huge vessel was reversing slowly away from the quayside and several other passengers appeared on deck, caught up in the excitement of the real start to their holiday. The ship moved effortlessly, slowed, turned towards the harbour mouth and with a grace belying its size headed for open sea, waves splashing gently against her bow. They were off. Beth glanced at the seal as they sailed past. It was still looking mournful. She was feeling a lot better. Ryan glanced at his watch.

'Well they're certainly on time. I didn't realise it was as late as that. I'd love to stay and talk,' he said in a soft captivating tone, 'but I think perhaps we'd best be getting back to the cabin, eh?'

Siobhán looked up at Beth apologetically: 'Unfortunately it takes me longer to get ready these days.' Her shoulders lifted and she waved her hands in a helpless gesture.

Beth saw the flicker of anguish pass across Siobhán's face. The emotional turmoil she'd suffered herself bore no comparison to whatever it was this girl had been through. She felt guilty for her self-pity; guilty for envying Siobhán because she had Ryan.

'Take as long as you need, Siobhán. I promise we won't start without you.'

Beth followed them with her eyes as they made their way below. She felt something stir deep inside, unsought and for the moment at least unwanted, a something she'd thought never to experience again and certainly not so soon after the last fiasco. Ryan was strictly off limits. How on earth was she going to get through the next fourteen days, seeing him every day with someone else? It seemed the ship she'd hoped would be her escape might end up being her prison.

* ★ ★

Ryan gave Siobhán as much help as he could before himself showering and getting dressed. He could sense her watching him as he dried his hair.

'Look at this, Siobhán. Even the towels match the décor. Everything in this cabin screams luxury.'

'What were you expecting? A hammock?'

He'd spent hours researching online, looking for somewhere to take her, to get her away, somewhere to help her forget. *If only I could.* A cruise offered the best option. Disabled people — the thought came unasked into his head — were well catered for on ocean liners. And at least she'd have the chance to see some of the places she'd always dreamed of, albeit from the confines of her wheelchair. He watched her fixing her hair but his thoughts were elsewhere.

'Something on your mind, Ryan? You look as if you're a million miles away.'

'No, only in the hundreds. I was just hoping the crossing from Dublin to Liverpool and driving half the length of England wasn't too much for you.'

'Bless your heart, I'm a bit tired for sure but there's no way I'm going to miss this evening's entertainment. I expect I shall sleep like a babe tonight though.'

Ryan hadn't been altogether honest with Siobhán because he most certainly did have something on his mind: a five-foot, two-inch curly-haired blonde with a figure that men die for and women diet for — and he'd only met her an hour since. In the circumstances sharing his thoughts with Siobhán wouldn't have been the kindest thing to do, but he couldn't banish Beth from his mind or the way she'd blushed when he'd teased her about the cruise. With all that was going on in his life this wasn't the time to be getting involved with anyone, but he could feel sensations stirring him in a way he was helpless to control. His conscience spoke to him loud and clear.

What about the promise you made to yourself after Siobhán's accident? What about the promise you made to her? 'I'll devote myself to you for as long as you need me, Siobhán. For as long as it takes.' That's what you said.

And I meant what I said, Ryan replied to his inner voice. *It doesn't mean I can't have feelings.*

Just as long as you keep them under wraps. Siobhán needs you, now more than ever.

As if he didn't know.

Ryan tried to think of something other than Beth. The girl was playing havoc with his inner peace. He sat on the bed with his back against the soft cream pillows, of which there was an abundance, and grabbed a handful of brochures. He waved the itinerary at Siobhán.

'Two full days at sea, then first stop Gibraltar, where Europe meets Africa. What a picture that conjures up, eh?'

'Yes, we certainly have some treats in

store for us. It's just a shame you'll miss so many of the beauty spots en route, Ryan. As you can imagine, I don't feel great about it. I can't help thinking I'm a burden.'

'What utter bull, Siobhán. First and foremost this holiday is for you, remember. In any case I'd never get the chance to see half the things ahead of us if it weren't for you.'

'Weren't for my accident you mean.'

Ryan leapt off the bed and sank to his knees in front of her. 'The accident wasn't your fault. No, don't interrupt me. You are going to get better. They've told you the damage isn't permanent. You just have to give it time. And while you do we're going to explore places neither of us ever expected to see. And because they cater so well for people in your circumstances . . . '

Siobhán flinched.

'Yes, I know you don't want to listen but you have to be realistic. That's why we've booked the excursions; they know all the potential hazards and they'll deal

11

with them for us. We'll be in safe hands.' He gripped her own clenched hands. 'We have to make the best of it, Siobhán. It's what Niall would have wanted; Caitlan too.'

'You're right; I know you're right. And I'm so sorry to be such a pain when you've gone to such lengths to make this work for me.'

'That's better. Now, finish off your make-up, put some of that blusher stuff on your cheeks and let's go party.'

2

Beth stood nervously in a reception area that promoted the peace and opulence of the ship, decorated as it was in the company's trademark colours of cream and soft powder blue. Her mother would certainly have envied the drapes, had she seen them, though the light fittings were perhaps a bit ostentatious for the average domestic sitting room. Her anxiety wasn't because she was worried about the job; she was wondering if Ryan had noticed how much she'd been thrown off balance that afternoon. She'd laughed at Claire's text which she'd finally read back in her cabin.

'What do you mean, Adonis? What do you mean, Later? I want to know Now!'

'The most beautiful man in the whole world.'

Beth expected Claire to send another message but instead her phone rang.

'Okay, out with it.'

'He was there, on the deck. A vision with a voice that would make your toes curl.'

'Oh cruel world. It should have been me.'

'One tiny drawback. He's married.'

But for Beth, in spite of her comment, it wasn't tiny at all; it was huge.

Though she didn't tell Claire, she knew Ryan had touched her deeply and it was going to take all her self-control to hide it from him. Her working face usually masked her inner thoughts but he'd certainly caught her off guard earlier in the day. It was back in place now as she waited to greet the guests. She may never have been on a ship before but back home she spent her working life co-ordinating and promoting events, and meeting and greeting important people at business conventions; she could almost do it with her eyes closed, and Claire's recommendation had been enough to land her the job. With her friend so suddenly laid low she rather thought they needed her as much as she needed them. Simon, her boss, relied on her totally for the outward facing side of the business — and much of the inward facing as well — but he'd been happy enough though to let her take a couple of weeks leave at short notice. He knew about Gerry and in any case she'd been a bit run-down recently.

'No problem. The sea air will do you good.'

No, her apprehension arose from the anticipated meeting with Ryan. Her reaction to him on deck had been instinctive and she tried to kid herself it was because she wasn't in working mode. *I'll be okay now — forewarned is forearmed.* It was a rather vain hope. Beth studied the passenger list on her clipboard, knowing it wouldn't be long before she would be able to put a face to every name. It was just one of those quirky things she'd been lucky to be born with, that and the fact she got a lot of practice. There were two names she was certain she'd never have to struggle to remember: Ryan and Siobhán Donovan.

Flanked by waiters wearing powder-blue waistcoats with matching ties and holding trays of champagne cocktails and crudités, Beth waited to receive the holidaymakers. There was a general buzz of anticipation in the room as people got ready to enjoy their first evening on board. The excitement was almost tangible. She could have done with a cocktail herself as Ryan manoeuvred Siobhán's chair towards her through the throng. Perhaps it was just as well she didn't have one. She was trembling so much she'd probably have spilled half of it on the floor or, worse still, on his beautifully polished shoes. She raised her eyes to his and was even more disturbed to find herself gazing into pools of chestnut-brown that stared intently back at her.

'Welcome aboard, Mr Don — '

'Oh no, not so formal, Beth. We've already met remember and I'm hoping we're going to become great friends. First names, please.'

The twinkle she'd seen that afternoon was back, only it was stronger even than she remembered. Beth had heard the expression 'laughing eyes', but this was the first time she'd actually seen them. For a moment she didn't have a word to say until she told herself sternly, *Pull yourself together. You've got a job to do.*

'Siobhán, Ryan, it's good to see you again.' She smiled warmly and handed a drink to Siobhán as Ryan helped himself from a proffered tray.

'You'll not be having one yourself then?'

Beth felt her heart lurch as she heard the soft lilt in his voice. It wasn't fair that one man was not only outrageously attractive but also possessed a voice that held the promise of, well, all the things she needed to stop herself thinking about. She hadn't felt like this since she was a teenager.

'Later. When I've made sure all the names have been ticked off my list and everyone is enjoying themselves.'

'Sure, you can tick me off. Any time. May I join you? When you've accounted for everyone, that is.'

That inflection again, like soft warm toffee. Folds of velvet fluttered around in her stomach as he spoke, like sand disturbed by a gentle flow of desert air. *And is he flirting with me?* She glanced down at Siobhán, trying to conjecture what she was making of all this, and was relieved to see her looking around the room, apparently detached from the conversation. Beth told herself it was just his Irish blarney, and smiled back.

'Of course. I'll look forward to it,' she said, and look forward to it she would; whether or not she could handle it in a professional manner was another question.

Ryan and Siobhán moved away to make room for the next guests and

Beth didn't see either of them again until after she'd greeted everyone and had a moment to look around. Siobhán's wheelchair was standing in the frame of a huge floor-to-ceiling window dressed in cream silk drapes with blue piping. *She looks so beautiful in that backdrop. I wonder what happened to her.* A couple of passengers had drawn their own chairs up to hers and the three were deep in conversation. Of Ryan there was no sign. Beth picked him out immediately in the dining room — he wasn't easy to miss — but she looked away when she saw him watching her.

After dinner when there were so many demands on her time there was little opportunity for proper conversation. She could only be grateful this first meal was informal and it hadn't fallen to her turn to sit at their table as the captain's rota would have her do at some later stage. How would she cope spending an evening in close proximity to this man who had overturned her composure? Perhaps with time she'd be able to control the feelings that flared up inside her every time she thought about him. She doubted it though.

* * *

Ryan was having his own problems, having failed miserably to contrive more than a few moments in Beth's company. Back in his cabin he was mulling over his ineptitude when his sister said: 'Why don't you go and have a nightcap? It said in the programme they have a pianist in the main bar every evening.'

'You must be joking. I'm not leaving you here in the cabin on your own, Siobhán!'

'I'm not a child, you know. I'll be fine, Ryan, honestly. I can do my own clothes and the wheelchair goes in easily next to the wall. It's only my legs that don't work. I'll heave myself onto the bed when I'm ready.'

'I don't know . . . but, if you're sure;

if you think you can manage,' Ryan said doubtfully, perceived responsibility vying with the need to see Beth again.

'With that wonderful meal on top of all the travelling I can barely keep my eyes open.'

'You certainly looked as if you were enjoying the cucumber and truffle Carpaccio.'

'Well I didn't see you holding back on the filet mignon either.'

'No, it was superb. Best I've ever had, I think. Mind you, it was difficult making a decision with such a variety of things to choose from. I don't know how they do it with so many people to look after.'

'Look, if it'll make you feel any better hang on while I get undressed. I'm in the middle of a good book but I don't think I'll even be able to focus on that. You can tuck me in then go on and enjoy yourself.'

He knew she meant it and allowed himself to be pulled where he wanted to go. Without further argument and waiting only to see her settled, Ryan made his way to the bar to find a few other passengers relaxing at the end of what had been a very long day. He looked around hopefully and was rewarded with a glimpse of Beth tucked away in the corner and almost hidden from view by a couple who had been sitting at his table during dinner. The restaurant had by no means been full, as several of the passengers had chosen informal dining for their first night on board, but their companions had declared they liked being pampered from the word go. Ryan and Siobhán had picked it as the easy option until they had an opportunity to familiarise themselves with the ship's layout.

Now he knew Beth was there, Ryan took the time to order a drink. 'Would you have any Irish Whiskey behind there?'

'Of course, Sir. Would you be wanting ice with that?'

'And ruin a beautiful drink? Certainly not,' he said, smiling. He rested his elbow on the bar while he waited, seemingly relaxed but in fact anxious not to foul things up by rushing in headlong. After a few moments, drink in hand, he moved across the room between armchairs and sofas, unconsciously stroking the material with his fingertips as he went. He went towards Beth, using Bob and Sally as his pretext.

'What a great meal that was, eh, Sally? If that's where they're setting the standard I am prepared to enjoy myself immensely.'

'It's all right for you men, particularly those of you the size of a small building. You can hide a couple of pounds here and there and it doesn't even show. I've got my waistline to think about. Life is so unfair.'

'Well it's a very pretty waistline for sure. I'd think about it myself if Bob wasn't standing here. I don't believe you have too much to worry about.'

'You're outrageous, Ryan. Did you hear that, Bob? Ryan's commenting on my figure. I can't remember the last time you did that.'

'He's Irish, Sally. They're always ready with a pretty word. Not,' he added quickly, 'that you don't have a good figure.'

'Great recovery, Bob,' Ryan said. 'Very impressive.'

'Don't mind me, will you. I don't care if the pair of you stand there discussing my attributes.'

Beth, listening to their chitchat, couldn't help reflecting that it wasn't Ryan's waistline she was thinking about. Even with his superbly cut jacket on there was no hiding the muscles that rippled underneath. She tried unsuccessfully to get a grip on herself.

'What have you done with Siobhán? Is she okay?' Bob asked.

'Just a bit tired after all the travelling. She sent me up here so she could get an early-ish night. I don't think she'll be counting too many sheep before she drops off.' He looked down at Beth where she'd sunk into an armchair.

'Mind if I join you? I could do with sitting down myself. It feels like days since we left Dublin.'

What could she do? To say no would be rude. To get up and leave would be rude. Was it no-win or win-win? She wasn't sure. Ryan took her silence as acquiescence and sat beside her.

'It's okay for you youngsters. Sally and I are going to follow Siobhán's example. It's the sea air; seasoned travellers though we are, it does this to us every time, at the beginning anyway. Night.'

'Night, Bob. Sally.'

'Night.'

Ryan leaned back in the chair, one long leg folded loosely over the other. Beth could have no idea how hard it had been for him to maintain the small talk with Sally and Bob when all he wanted to do was be alone with her. He looked at her through smouldering eyes, battling with himself to take his time. Whatever it was he saw spurred him on; and with the air of somebody treading on eggshells, but determined to continue, he took his fate firmly in his hands.

'You must have realised how I feel about you — from the moment I saw you on deck this afternoon?' He came straight to the point, then, sweeping everything else aside. No way to pretend she didn't understand.

So much for getting a grip, she thought. 'But we've only just met. You can't — '

'Sure I was thinking maybe you felt the same way. There's all my hopes gone; dashed to the ground beneath those pretty feet.'

His words were light but there was no mistaking the sincerity behind them. Molten lava took the place of where her stomach should have been as her body experienced yet another new sensation. Her response was immediate and spontaneous. She put her hand out to cover his where it rested lightly on the arm of the chair — they might as well have slept together, so strong was the explosion between them. Beth, suddenly remembering Siobhán, put her free hand to one burning cheek. Ryan leaned forward and stroked the other with his fingertip, shielding her from view with his body as he moved in front of her.

'I want to be alone with you, Beth.'

'Ryan, this is insane. We can't. I can't.'

'Now I was raised to believe there's no such word as can't, not that I think this is what me mam and dad meant at the time. To be sure we'd cause a sensation if I followed my instincts right here and now. Truth is, Beth, sometimes magic happens when you're least expecting it. Don't tell me you don't feel it too. I won't believe you.'

'But you're — '

'No buts. I know the reasoning but reason has no place here. It is what it is.'

Her whole body fired up in answer and he knew. Whatever it was, this new thing, it was there for both of them. Suddenly his sophistication deserted him and he pleaded with her, his voice rasping, 'Meet me on deck, where I first saw you this afternoon. Please, Beth. Please.'

He threw the remains of his drink down his aching throat and left.

3

Beth sat for a while, her mind in confusion, her body reacting in a way she wouldn't have believed possible that morning. How could she feel this way when — was it only this morning she had been bitter and broken? How Gerry would have scorned her if he knew that but for Siobhán she would be contemplating . . . yes, she really would be contemplating giving herself without reservation to someone she'd met only that day.

And what does that make me? She wasn't sure she liked the answer. Her attachment to Gerry had been genuine enough, but even in the beginning she'd never experienced the intensity she was feeling now for Ryan. She was starting to realise that what she'd felt for Gerry paled into insignificance when compared with the emotion generated by

Ryan with just a lift of his eyebrow.

Beth and Gerry had been living together for well over a year, but it had often felt like she was being pushed into a place she wasn't sure she wanted to be. Strange for such an independent spirit, but she'd so wanted the romance — and she had to admit Gerry had been good at romance when he'd wanted to be. With Ryan she was beginning to believe in something she'd always scoffed at. Love at first sight.

'I won't share,' she had told Gerry. So what was she doing even letting herself think about the man who with one glance had cured her of the two-timing bastard who'd deceived her for so long? Would she be any better than Gerry if she met Ryan while his wife lay sleeping alone in their cabin?

How could she even contemplate meeting him? What sort of a person was she? Regardless of what her body was telling her he wasn't free. Had she just pulled out of one triangle only to plunge headlong into another? She couldn't do it. Beth went to bed.

★ ★ ★

'You didn't come. I waited but you didn't come.'

Ryan had run Beth to ground next morning on the top deck where she was overseeing the mini-golf. Looking for an opportunity to break in, he nevertheless felt the need to proceed with caution. Though he was happy enough for Beth to see his unashamed feelings for her, he had no faith in his ability to hide this overwhelming desire from the rest of the world. Under different circumstances it wouldn't have bothered him in the least, but he didn't want to put her in a difficult position. This wasn't a holiday for her, it was a job; and if he'd understood correctly, she was new to it. There must be all sorts of regulations about staff mixing with passengers. For once in his life he was being circumspect.

His chance came when there was an

announcement that the guest speaker was about to begin a lecture in the theatre on the history of Gibraltar. There was a mass exodus and suddenly they were alone except for someone sleeping on a sunbed some distance to the fore and well out of earshot.

'Ryan, I couldn't. What sort of a person would I be if I got mixed up with someone else's husband? It's why I left my last relationship.' She added somewhat bitterly, 'After nearly two years I found out he had a wife.'

Ryan looked puzzled, then a smile slowly formed on his handsome face, widening to a grin and finally erupting into a delightful and delighted chuckle. It was Beth's turn to be puzzled.

'I don't understand. What's so funny?'

'Siobhán? She's my sister, Beth, not my wife.'

'But you're sharing a cabin with her. You can't — '

'Like I said, she's my sister. We've been naked in front of each other ever since the day she was born. Don't you have any brothers or sisters?'

'Sadly, no.'

'Well, we both know how to turn our backs when necessary, but even with a disabled cabin she needs my help to fetch and carry, when she takes a shower, or has difficulty reaching her clothes. It was because of the facilities that we decided on a cruise. The doors are wider, there's a ramp to the bathroom, a roll-in shower and, well, lots of extras, including a balcony. It doesn't come cheap, but fortunately we're in a position where we could do it, and Siobhán's health and peace of mind are the priority here. I'm sorry, Beth; perhaps I should have made it clear to begin with. It never crossed my mind you'd . . . ' By which time he was laughing so much he couldn't even finish the sentence.

Beth was delighted and her ready grin, always near the surface, spread across her face. She'd begun to think she'd left one two-timing bastard only to meet another one. Her faith in men had been badly shaken and it was fantastic to discover it wasn't what she'd thought. He was free. She could follow her heart with an easy conscience. He could feel the change in her; watched as the tension left her body, his own completely relaxed now he knew the reason for her no show.

'Dammit, Beth, we're standing here in broad daylight and someone could come up the stairway at any moment. I have to see you alone. I have to or I'll burst.' Not so relaxed after all.

She giggled at the inference and once more felt herself responding to him. More at ease now, she teased him. 'I'm on duty all day, Ryan. Then there's the captain's first formal dinner tonight, followed by dancing. I can't wait to see you in your dinner suit.'

'And I can't wait for you to see me out of it. Tonight then? After dinner? Are you allowed to dance with the passengers?'

'Allowed to, yes, but I'm not sure it's

such a good idea. I don't think either of us will prove to be very good at hiding — well, you know.'

'That's for sure; and I'd better not come anywhere near you wearing swimming trunks either. Later then. God, I'll be glad when we get to Gibraltar and I can get off this ship and do something.'

She looked a bit surprised at this somewhat unexpected turn in the conversation. 'I thought you were impressed with the facilities.'

'I am. What I'm not impressed with is seeing you and not being able to lay a finger on you.' His beautiful smile dawned again and his voice slowed almost to a standstill. 'Then another finger, and another, then . . . '

'Stop it, Ryan. I'm having difficulty enough just standing here. You'd better go before I lose my judgement and with it my job.'

Ryan cast a quick look at the sleeping passenger, thought better of his impulse to take her in his arms and went below in search of Siobhán. They hadn't even touched.

Aside from the unexpected though now not unwelcome complication of Ryan, Beth was enjoying the cruise. Her role wasn't anywhere near as demanding as she'd thought it would be. The ship was a well-oiled machine, structurally and socially. She smiled every time she thought of her encounter with Ruth and Lydia the previous day as she'd begun familiarising herself with the layout.

'Come in. Come in. She's beating me hollow and a distraction is just what I need,' invited a lady with immaculate blue-rinsed hair as Beth had put her head round the door of the card room. Thus summoned, she stepped inside to find two women playing Scrabble. Hard to tell how old they were but neither would see seventy again.

'Don't you dare! She's always pulling

tricks like that,' said her companion, with an equally unbelievably coloured coiffure, though hers was bright red and in stark contrast to her perfect out-of-a-bottle complexion. Beth realised the rejection wasn't for real and advanced towards them.

'I thought all the passengers had disembarked. I'm assuming you're not members of staff.'

'Back-to-back,' said Blue Rinse.

'I'm sorry; I don't understand.'

'Back-to-back cruises. When you get to our age it's what we do, those of us who've been left a fortune by our husband, whose children only want to see us three times a year and who would rather be waited upon than sit in splendid isolation at home, dining in for one.' Henna Lady didn't seem the least bit put out by her description. 'Where else could we find a handsome thirty-something willing to stand up with us on the dance floor and pretend it's the one place on earth he most wants to be?'

Beth was delighted. 'Well, if you make them smile the way you have me I'm certain pretence has nothing to do with it. If I were a man I'd dance with you myself. I'm Beth; ship's hostess. First time round for me,' Beth said, wondering why she felt the compulsion to tell them.

'You come to us then, if you need any pointers. We've done it so many times we've lost count. I'm Ruth,' said Blue Rinse, 'and this is Lydia.'

'Thank you. I will, and it's been lovely meeting you.'

Beth had left the room chuckling to herself. *And I was under the impression entertaining was supposed to be my job.*

★　★　★

Looking forward to the evening, Beth was very grateful there were no mind-readers to see beyond her outwardly composed appearance. Several passengers kept to their cabins during the afternoon as the Bay of Biscay chose to be somewhat less than tranquil. The turbulence wasn't excessive but was uncomfortable enough to empty the public areas of a fair percentage of the population. She saw Ryan only fleetingly when he sought her out to explain that Siobhán was feeling a little unwell.

'Although she doesn't want me holding her hand, it's spooked her. It reminds her a bit of the accident. I don't want to leave her alone.' He hurried away without elaborating and Beth found herself wondering what had caused his sister's injuries. She hoped the time would come when he would confide in her.

Beth spent much of the day reassuring people the disturbance would be short-lived and the gentler waters of the Mediterranean were not too far away, something she knew little about but was pretty sure would be the case. Truth to tell, the stabilisers were doing their job, but unfortunately there were some for whom any motion was unsettling. Luckily she wasn't one of them, though; this had been her one fear when she'd accepted the job. The Isle of Wight ferry was her only previous experience of travelling on water — well, that and the occasional rowing boat on the Isis, which she didn't really think counted.

Once she'd satisfied herself she'd done everything she could for those in her care she made her way to one of the decks where she could easily be found via her walkie-talkie if needed and settled down to read. Though she was unaffected by the motion of the ship, the turmoil raging within her was heightened. Completely unable to concentrate on her book and with no other distractions, she allowed her thoughts to focus on the man with thick curly hair and twinkling eyes whose image filled every moment. A vivid imagination conjured up a picture of this muscled Adonis in swimming trunks — *well, he was the one who put the idea into my head* — and which she tried unsuccessfully to eliminate; moreover, she found herself dwelling on it with considerable pleasure. And that wasn't all. Last night she'd even dreamt about him. She phoned Claire.

'Adonis is a bachelor.'

'But you said . . . '

'I was wrong.'

'And to think it could have been me.'

'You wouldn't like him. He's well over six feet tall. It would set off that funny spot in your neck if you had to keep looking up.'

'If he's that good I'd be prepared to suffer. Or stand on a box. Have fun.'

Beth was smiling as Claire ended the call. It was hard to believe that yesterday morning she hadn't even been aware of Ryan's existence.

4

Ryan looked up to find Siobhán watching him affectionately as he got ready for dinner. He smiled back at her. 'How's your tummy? Are you feeling any better?'

'Yes and I'm looking forward to a good meal. I haven't eaten all day and I'm really hungry.' Her stomach rumbled as if to prove her point.

Ryan, sublimely unconscious of his own attractiveness, was taking more than usual care over his appearance.

'Aren't you just the real thing,' she teased him. 'Sure there's no lady will be able to resist you tonight.'

'That's enough of that, my girl. I'm already escorting the most beautiful woman on the ship. Why would I want anyone else?'

Ryan was hoping Siobhán hadn't noticed the change in him. Beth had thought his sister was unaware of the fire between her and Ryan, but they were both wrong.

'So you'll not be leaving my side this evening to spend some time with a certain diminutive blond of our acquaintance?'

'Oh my Lord, is it that obvious?'

'Only to me, Ryan, but then I have known you all my life. I'm absolutely thrilled. It's the best thing that could have happened to you. I'm not the only one who lost family in the accident, and you've had to be strong for both of us. It's time you thought about yourself for a change. Mind you, you look even taller than ever walking as you are two feet above the ground. Be careful though. I've never seen you so fired up over anyone before.'

'Nor have I ever been, Siobhán. She's with me every second, in my mind, in my heart and in places a brother shouldn't tell his sister about.'

'Spare me the details. As long as you put me somewhere I can enjoy watching the dancing there is no compulsion for you to stick by my side this evening. Just remember to come back for me before they play the last waltz. I'd feel very silly sitting there on my own.'

'I was rather hoping to get you tucked safely up in bed before I make a move. God, it sounds so calculated, doesn't it? But I'm not sure I can be trusted to control myself in front of a room full of people. Aside from which, I can hardly ask Beth to wait for me while I escort you to our cabin. It'd be like pouring cold water on her from a great height. She'd be quite right telling me to get lost.'

'There's little chance of that, I think, what with the pair of you smelling of April and May, but you've known lots of girls. You know how to handle yourself.'

'It never mattered so much before, Siobhán. It's been barely a day and already I know I want to spend the rest of my life with her.'

'She really has hit you hard, hasn't she?'

'I feel like an adolescent in the throes of first love. I can't take the risk of cocking it up.'

They both laughed at this in the circumstances rather unfortunate choice of words. Ryan dropped an affectionate kiss on the top of her head.

'Come on, then, sis. Let's do it,' he said, and wheeled her deftly out of the cabin and along to the dining room.

* * *

Beth took her place at the entrance to the dining room, receiving each guest as they arrived and handing every woman a red rose 'with the compliments of the captain'. Siobhán smiled so warmly up at her as she took the flower that Beth had little doubt brother had confided in sister. She raised a charmingly flushed face to greet the cause of her discomfiture and wasn't helped when he said, 'A rose to match the bloom in

45

your cheeks.' Fortunately anyone who might have overheard would have put his comment down to 'the Irish', but she knew there was more to it than that. He might be flirting with her outrageously and in a way that was perfectly socially acceptable, but Beth's blood pounded harder than ever, even as she knew his was doing.

'Enough of your blarney, Mr Donovan,' she responded, but there was a warning in her eyes. It was going to be a long night. Beth made good use of the time during dinner to regain her composure only to lose it immediately when Ryan approached her in the ballroom. She'd been sitting talking to Ruth and Lydia, both of whom with the shrewd eyes of age and experience had noticed the interest between the two. Ruth, who sported a sense of humour as blue as her hair, nudged Beth and whispered something that caused her to turn almost as bright a red as the one crowning Lydia's head.

'Good evening, ladies. Allow me to

introduce myself. I'm Ryan Donovan.'

'I'm Ruth; and this — ' She gestured to her friend. ' — is Lydia. No need I'm sure to acquaint you with Beth here.'

'No indeed. We all met her at the reception, did we not? And may I have the pleasure of this dance?'

Ruth was on her feet with a speed which belied her years. 'Of course, young man; I'd be delighted.'

Ryan was delighted too, admiring her alacrity and her sense of humour. He took great pleasure in whirling her around the floor (though slowly) and chuckling all the while before returning her to her seat, thanking her formally. He then asked Lydia if she, too, would do him the honour. 'And I hope you will join me when we come back, Beth,' he added, thus ensuring she stayed where she was till he claimed her.

Such a quizzical look there was in his eye, and little she could have done to refuse even if she'd wanted to. Ruth and Beth watched as Ryan and Lydia waltzed away. She was surprisingly nimble and it was a pleasure to watch the dance performed with such precision and grace.

'You'll have to watch that one, Beth. He's after you, that's for sure. I hope you didn't mind me stepping in like that; it was far too good an opportunity to miss.'

'No, it was nice to see you put into practice what you told me in the card room. You're a rogue, Ruth, but it was wonderful watching you in action. Do you give formal lessons?'

The two were still laughing when Ryan and Lydia came back and he claimed Beth for the next dance. She stepped willingly and for the first time into his arms. It was the most natural thing on earth. Home at last. A shudder of pure joy went through her whole body and she could feel Ryan's response, holding her tightly against him, urging her, daring her.

'You said you would wait; that we wouldn't dance together.'

'I'm done with waiting, Beth. I could

no more have stood by this evening and watched you than stopped breathing of my own accord. Can't you feel how much I need you?'

She missed her step and indeed she was aware of the tension in every muscle in his body. Had it not been for the support of his strong arms enfolding her she would certainly have stumbled. He held her as if she was the most precious thing in the world and as far as he was concerned that's what she was.

'Now I know what people mean when they say their knees have buckled. Don't let go of me, Ryan.'

'If I have my way I'll never let go of you again.'

What magic had happened that they both felt this way? Beth wondered. So much, so soon. Preliminaries weren't necessary. They just knew. They might have been at sea, but in Ryan's arms she felt as if she'd reached a safe harbour.

'We have to get through this. When

this dance is over I have to circulate. I can't spend the whole evening with you; it's more than my job is worth.'

'Damn your job . . . ' he protested, though he realised he was being selfish. 'No, you're right. I'm not being fair, but I can't wait much longer, sweetheart. Will you meet me on deck later, when all this is over?'

'What about Siobhán?'

'We have her blessing. Oh Beth, this is agony,' he groaned in her ear.

Fortunately for them both the dance came to an end and somehow they were able to disentangle without drawing attention to themselves.

'I'll be there, same place as before,' she whispered as she turned away.

The rest of the evening passed in a haze for Beth. Luckily her actions and responses were automatic. Once in a while she glanced at the ornate clock that graced one of the walls. Were the hands really moving that slowly? It felt as if they weren't moving at all. Eventually people drifted away and

Beth watched as Ryan wheeled his sister out of the ballroom. Was it her imagination, or did Siobhán give her a little wave as they left? Even then the minutes seemed to stretch on until the room finally was empty of all except members of staff or crew.

Beth took a deep breath and made her way on deck. He was waiting for her, and even with her own heightened feelings she smiled to see him pacing up and down. Ryan turned, saw her and opened his arms. With something between a laugh and a cry she ran the last two steps towards him. He gathered her to him greedily. She rose on tiptoe to meet him but he retreated, holding her at arm's length. The hunger was laid bare in his eyes and she knew he was trembling, as she was. He looked down at her for several moments longer, as if he couldn't get enough, then lowered his lips to hers — and stopped.

'Beth, oh Beth.' The huskiness in his voice with that wonderful Irish lilt reached deep inside her to a place she didn't even know was there. He smoothed the hair away from her forehead and traced the line of her eyebrow with his finger. Even at this slight touch her breath became ragged. She waited, afraid to move, desperate not to break the spell. Ryan stroked her burning cheek. He took her chin between finger and thumb, searching her eyes. Satisfied with what he found there, he smiled.

He moved his hand to her waist and shifted his body weight. She gasped and he leaned towards her, brushing her lips gently with his own. He brushed them again and then, urgently now, pressed his mouth against hers, forcing her lips apart with his tongue, searching, seeking, demanding. The answer was there waiting for him as her mouth responded to his, her tongue answering his own. Their first kiss. How long they remained there neither knew, until a breeze from the water caused Beth to shiver.

'You're cold.'

'Hardly that,' she answered, but he took off his jacket and put it around her. They moved to the rail and gazed out onto the sea where small white horses cantered across the surface, gleaming in the moonlight. There they stood, shoulder to shoulder, each wanting more but content for the time being just to be together, and together they watched the sun rise.

5

The waters were calmer and the sun shone down on the *Mediterranean Adventurer*, bathing her occupants in gentle warmth. In the sea for which the liner was named temperatures would be higher, but here in the Atlantic several of the passengers described it as pleasant. It would serve to acclimatise them for what was to come. A good number were already gathered around the pool.

Beth had been doing a tour of duty. She'd visited the public areas inside and found two or three people in the library so lost in their books they didn't even look up, so she left without disturbing them. There were two rubbers of bridge and a game she didn't recognise in progress in the card room. Waiting only to make sure all was well, she retreated, knowing the card players at least wouldn't thank her for the intrusion. The decks were scattered with people revelling in this first perfect day, an ample supply of umbrellas shielding those who wished from the sun. Yesterday's uncomfortable motion was a thing of the past and Beth was greeted with smiling faces wherever she went.

Having left the pool area until last, Beth made her way aft, marvelling at how much the ship had to offer and how lucky she was getting paid for being there. Sally waved at Beth from the comfort of her sun lounger.

'I'm hoping this unattractive shade of pink will turn to burnished bronze before the end of the holiday. Bob's gone to get a drink — no surprise there, eh? Look at him. The temptation's far too great what with the bar being right next to the pool.'

'We like to make it as easy as we can for our guests, Sally.'

'A bit too easy sometimes. Bob reckons he's getting enough exercise just walking the ten yards and back again. It's the same every trip. He won't make it to the gym until a couple of days before we're due home, by which time he'll be desperate to shed a pound or two. Of course it'll be far too late by then.'

Waiters were serving snacks as people abandoned themselves to the glorious day. Only a very few left the deck at lunchtime to eat in the restaurant. More than one would regret it later.

Ryan and Siobhán were side by side near the pool. Beth was happy to see the wheelchair folded and out of the way and assumed Ryan had lifted his sister onto the sunbed. There were no scars; no external evidence of her accident. Siobhán looked like any other beautiful young woman enjoying her holiday. As luck would have it the lounger next to Ryan was vacant and Beth felt free to join them for a few minutes, promising herself she would linger no longer than she had with any of the other passengers.

'Isn't this weather amazing! After yesterday it's so nice to see everyone enjoying the sunshine.'

Ryan, lying face down, hadn't seen her approach. At the sound of her voice — friendly and business-like now and far removed from the husky tones he'd engendered in her last night — he raised his head from where it had been resting on his arms and turned to look at her. The electricity crackled between them, so powerful Beth wondered if it was audible. The smile dawned again, the eyes laughed.

'Sure it's beautiful. Mind you, the sun's a bit fierce. While you're here would you mind rubbing some cream into my back?' he said, passing her the bottle.

The cheek of the man. Well, she'd call his bluff.

'Of course I will. All part of the service.' She poured some of the cool white lotion onto the palm of her hand and made circular movements on Ryan's shoulders and back, smoothing it into his skin. It was an apparently innocent enough occupation and nobody else heard him groan or the words that followed: 'Thanks be to my personal saint that I'm face down. Did I not tell you it wouldn't be a good idea — you, me and swimming trunks?'

'Have you no control?' She smiled, enjoying his discomfiture.

'Not where you're concerned, Beth, no. Go and talk to Siobhán or I'll never be able to leave this sunbed.' She accepted his dismissal in good part, particularly as he followed this command with: 'I'll see you later.' Few words but filled with meaning.

Beth moved to the other side of Siobhán. There was a light in the young woman's eyes, not unlike that of her brother; how had she not noticed it before?

'Did you hear . . . ?'

'Not a word; didn't need to. Don't worry,' she said, smiling at Beth's anxious question, 'your secret's safe with me, and no one else would suspect a thing. Foreknowledge is a great asset. Be kind to him, Beth. He's been through a lot. Almost as much as me.'

'I hope to make it my life's work, being kind to him.' And she meant it.

★ ★ ★

'Songs from the Shows — A Musical Extravaganza': that's how the entertainment for the evening was billed, the first of several scheduled presentations in the huge theatre. Not everyone on the ship was a show-goer, of course, but the facilities had to be there just in case. Beth stood at the entrance at 5.30p.m., ready to receive the audience.

'They've thought of everything, haven't they,' Ryan observed as she showed them to their places where an aisle seat had been removed to accommodate the wheelchair. Professional as Beth was, her composure deserted her when she made the mistake of looking up into his eyes. How could they shine and smoulder at the same time? It was so unfair. Beth moved unsteadily back to her post at the door.

When everyone was settled and the music began she took a seat at the back, preparing to enjoy herself. Instead she spent most of the time aware of nothing as much as Ryan's proximity and the heat that flared into her face every time he looked round, which he did. Often! At the end of the show Ryan took her elbow and pulled her to one side, demanding: 'When can I see you, Beth? Are you coming to the dining room, where I can at least catch a glimpse of you from time to time? A man could waste away, you know.'

Ryan was appealing and demanding, plaintive and forceful, charming and imperious. He had a lot of ammunition and he was using it all.

'You're not helping, Ryan. I have to stay here for the second performance. I'll just grab a sandwich in between shows.'

'Yes, I know you're tied up here, but I

mean it anyway — about seeing you. I was rather hoping for a continuing performance of our own,' he said provocatively, piercing her with those wonderful eyes that were made to drown in. Mentally she added 'irresistible' to his list of attributes.

'You are shameless. How about a nightcap in the bar, after you've eaten and I've watched the show again?'

'It's a date — and come to think of it why don't I give you my mobile number. That way you can text me any time you're free, even if it's just for a few minutes. I'll come to you wherever you are.'

Beth enjoyed the second show almost as much as the first. Almost! *It's only because I've just seen it and I know what's coming next*, she tried to fool herself. But she wasn't, not for a moment. She knew it was because half her mind — maybe a bit more than half — was on the anticipated meeting with the beautiful, funny man to whom amazingly she'd lost her heart. She kept looking at her phone and calling up his details. Even that was an exquisite pleasure.

At ten thirty she sent Ryan a message: 'On my way,' trying it out for size. It felt deliciously naughty. She made her way to the bar where Ryan was already sitting at a table in the corner — their table, where he'd declared himself that first night. A plate of food was waiting for her and it dawned on her that the earlier sandwich was no substitute for dinner.

'Is this for me, Ryan? You're a star. I didn't even realise I was hungry.'

'Well you told me earlier you were only going to be able to find time for a snack. I don't want you passing out on me later; not from hunger anyway.'

It wasn't fair. No one had a right to light up the room like he did or to be able to put so much suggestion into a couple of sentences. He ordered her a drink and she attacked her meal with relish.

'I love a woman with strong appetites.' He took her serviette and wiped the corner of her mouth. 'Careful. You're dribbling.'

Startled, she grabbed the linen from him and dabbed at her face. 'I'm not. Surely I'm not.'

Ryan laughed out loud. 'No, not really, and if you are I hope it's for me. Kind of a metaphor.'

Blue eyes gazed into brown ones.

'I think I've had enough to eat,' she said.

Suddenly the atmosphere had changed. He'd become serious. Intense. 'Let me come to your room, Beth. Please.'

She wasn't proof to his appeal; didn't want to be. '361. It's cabin 361.'

★   ★   ★

Beth left the bar first, leaving Ryan to follow a few minutes later. He waited as long as his aching body would let him, anxious not to draw attention to her, not to raise a question in anyone's mind. As bad luck would have it the lead singer from the evening's show chose just the moment Ryan was entering Beth's cabin to come out of her own. Heaven knew where she was going at that time of night, but the cat was now well and truly out of the bag. She smiled knowingly at him, so he smiled back as he went through the door. What else could he do?

His first words to Beth were an apology. 'I'm so sorry, sweetheart. It looks like our cover's been blown. I've just been seen by someone coming out of a cabin down the gangway. I should have been more careful.'

Beth was mortified but pragmatic. 'You could hardly come swathed in a black cloak and with a mask over your face. I can't be the first member of staff this has happened to and it's not likely you're the first passenger either. Let's just hope he — '

'She.'

'*She* keeps it to herself. If she's

leaving her cabin at this time of night she probably has her own rendezvous and is unlikely to say anything anyway. Why would she?'

The logic was inescapable but the mood was broken and, though Ryan looked longingly at it, the bed remained empty. Ryan and Beth went instead to one of the ship's lounges and spent an hour or so drinking coffee and talking.

' . . . so when I met him at the convention with another woman and discovered she was his wife, you can imagine how I felt. That was the last I saw of him. Lucky for me this job came up. I still can't believe it was only two days ago I was licking my wounds and swearing I'd never trust anyone again. That's why when I first saw you and Siobhán, I thought . . . well, you know what I thought. I just hope you don't have a wife hidden away somewhere.' She didn't raise her voice at the end of the sentence but the question was there nonetheless.

'Who my sister just happened to

forget to mention to you. No, Beth, no wife.'

The answer was straightforward enough but, though she couldn't be sure, Beth sensed a hesitation, something withheld as if there was more to follow; something deliberately left unsaid. Beth felt uneasy for the first time, but she couldn't believe all her instincts were wrong.

But he's Irish and he has the tongue.

But he also has the most honest eyes I've ever seen.

But I really don't know anything about him.

What do I need to know, other than that I love him?

But I loved Gerry too, and look what happened there.

She gave up the internal argument and asked if he and Siobhán were going ashore the next day.

'Yes, neither of us has been to Gibraltar before. We've booked a car with a private guide, although some of the later excursions are within our capabilities. We're hoping to see the apes. What about you? Are you staying on board?'

'No, I've got the day free. I'm going on the tour.'

'Can you come with us?' he asked eagerly.

'I think I'm expected to help out, even if it's unofficial.'

Ryan took Beth's hands in his own. She was trembling. 'Tomorrow, Beth. Tomorrow night. Can I see you then? I have to see you.'

There was no doubting the sincerity in his voice, but he was definitely troubled. All at once things were different between them. Beth couldn't rid herself of the feeling he was keeping something from her; it was as if an unbidden intruder had crept in while they weren't looking.

'It's my turn at your table for dinner tomorrow, Ryan. I'll see you then. Look at the time; I'd best be going. No, don't come with me,' she insisted as he stood up. 'Good night,' she said forlornly as she moved away, uncertainty intruding on her happiness. She realised, though she'd revealed so much about herself, that she knew nothing more about him than she had two hours ago.

6

The passengers were still sleeping as the cruise liner pulled into port. None saw the magnificent view of the Rock as the ship approached Gibraltar. By the time they were awake the *Mediterranean Adventurer* had dropped anchor and landing arrangements had been put in place. Ryan and Siobhán made contact with their driver, loaded the wheelchair and gave themselves into the care of their guide.

'Ryan, and Siobhán,' he said, indicating his sister and extending his hand in greeting.

'And I am Katrina,' their guide responded, taking his hand in her own. 'It's going to be a packed day. I hope you will like what I've chosen for you.'

It was a short trip to their first stop.

'Many of these animals have been seized from illegal traders,' Katrina said as they entered the wildlife conservation area of the Alameda Botanical Gardens. 'It won't ever be possible to release them. The income from the entry fee helps with the upkeep.'

'Oh look,' said Siobhán with delight, 'there's a baby. Is there any chance we can see the apes in the wild?' she asked.

'Certainly you can. The Apes Den is probably the most popular tourist attraction in Gibraltar and I'm planning to take you after lunch. I thought we'd have a stroll round the gardens first and a light snack before making our way there. Otherwise everything is done in such a rush it's impossible to take it all in.'

This was an irrefutable logic and their tour of the gardens got the thumbs-up from both of them. In fact it would have been difficult to judge whether brother or sister was the more excited.

'It's an absolute riot of colour. There are plants here I've never seen before; never even heard of. This one, for example,' said Ryan, pointing. '*Alpinia zerumbet*. It's stunning.'

'It's a member of the ginger family and not indigenous to Gibraltar, but it's a great favourite,' said Katrina. 'Porcelain-pink on the outside, but look — when it's open it's just begging to be pollinated.'

Katrina had arranged a simple meal in the garden café prior to them heading off to see Gibraltar's most famous inhabitants. Their guide kept up a seamless presentation, but they could feel her enthusiasm as she spoke.

'In spite of having no tails they aren't actually apes at all, they're monkeys — macaques — with almost as many legends surrounding them as there are monkeys themselves. There's a superstition that if they ever leave the Rock so too will the British. It's a bit like your own ravens at the Tower of London.'

The fact that they were Irish and it wasn't really their ravens or their Tower was lost on Katrina but they let

71

it go, not thinking it worth the explanation. The driver parked the car, scattering the macaques who, undeterred, returned moments later, so accustomed were they to their human visitors. There were hundreds of tourists milling around and they caught sight of a group of passengers from the *Adventurer*; though, try as he might, Ryan couldn't find Beth among the crowd. Even though he was captivated by everything around him he still couldn't get her out of his mind.

'What do they eat?' Siobhán asked.

'They're fed a supplement of fruit and vegetables and given fresh water daily, in addition to their main diet of leaves and other greenery.'

'That's probably part of the reason it's so whiffy here. It's not overwhelming but my goodness you can't miss it, can you?'

'We take the good with the bad. Some of us love them, some not so much,' Katrina replied, smiling.

'Are they monitored in any way?' Ryan wanted to know, dragging his attention back.

'Yes, every one of them is tattooed, micro-chipped, photographed and catalogued. During World War II their numbers dwindled to seven and believers of the legend were very concerned.'

'There's obviously no shortage of them now,' Siobhán remarked as three clambered onto the car looking for food.

'And they're always hungry. It's forbidden now to feed them, but with so many tourists and so many packed lunches they have become adept at stealing. You might be interested to know that apart from humans they are the only free living primates in Europe.'

Katrina's knowledge of Gibraltar seemed endless, and she entertained them with a steady stream of tales and historic facts on their journey back to the ship.

'In bygone times the Rock was considered to be one of the Pillars of

Hercules, and the system of caves and caverns was claimed to have been the entrance to Hades.'

'I can't believe how much you've managed to cram into one day. We've had a fabulous time and my sister and I will never forget our visit. Thank you.'

★ ★ ★

Beth's day hadn't been quite as happy and carefree as the Donovans'. To say her heart was troubled as she disembarked was a huge understatement. She was already vulnerable after her experience with Gerry. Though Ryan hadn't seen her at the Apes Den, she'd spotted him straight away. He looked so happy and so animated, and so bloody handsome! Feeling the need for some time away from him to sort out the turmoil in her mind and, yes, her heart, she moved behind the bus, out of his line of sight. The sun beat down on her back and at any other time she'd have soaked up the heat with enthusiasm.

Today, though, it was in stark contrast to the chill she was feeling inside. She waited there, subdued, all pleasure in these delightful animals gone until the car left and she was again able to relax a little.

Am I looking for a problem where none exists? She couldn't shake off the feeling he was holding something back.

The tour group had spent the morning visiting the spectacular natural caverns of St Michael's Cave. They'd walked the chambers, revealing giant stalactites and stalagmites, but the cold that Beth felt had nothing to do with the atmosphere in the cave. Their whistle-stop tour included a visit to the Moorish Castle before arriving at the Apes Den a little before Ryan and Siobhán. The coach had left the tourist attraction ten minutes behind their car and they arrived back some time after the couple had gone on board. Beth was relieved not to be meeting them again soon until she remembered she would have to endure dinner sitting at their table.

* * *

Beth almost jumped backwards when she entered her cabin. Someone else was already there. It took her a minute to remember she was sharing her accommodation from Gibraltar onwards.

'Sorry. I didn't mean to startle you. I'm Juanita, your roommate from now on.'

'No, of course. They told me when I arrived. I wasn't thinking.'

* * *

The two young women shook hands formally, then laughed simultaneously. Juanita continued: 'I don't know how much they told you about me.'

'Nothing, other than that we'd be in the same cabin. It feels as though I've been here for ages already and I've got so used to it, well, I suppose I just forgot.'

'I'm one of the entertainers, an opera singer. I took some leave after the last trip to come home and see my family.'

'Are you always in here? Have I taken the wrong bed?'

'No, we get moved around. I don't think I've ever been in this cabin before.'

'So do you live in Gibraltar?'

'Just across the border into Spain. I'm not due to go on for another couple of days so it wasn't problem. It's a dream of a job for me. Popular arias everyone knows and loves and the rest of the time off. What could be better?'

Beth went on to explain how she'd taken her place when Claire had been laid low with chicken pox and in no time the two chatting like old friends. Juanita spoke in a deep voice with a strong accent but her English was impeccable.

'I went to school in Gibraltar,' she explained, 'and to learn opera. I'm a contralto.'

Beth was keen to hear more about her fascinating roommate, but conscious of the time instead asked Juanita:

'Do you want the shower?'

'No, go ahead. I had one earlier. And thanks for leaving me enough wardrobe space when you did remember I was coming,' Juanita said, smiling. 'A couple of my gowns take up quite a lot of room.'

'I'd love to see them.'

'Now?'

'No, I'll wait until you're wearing them. I'm sure they'll look much better on you than on the hangers.'

Beth showered and dressed carefully, taking a great deal of time over her make-up.

She was talking to Sally when she caught sight of Ryan pushing his sister towards the table. Beth watched with a lump in her throat as Ryan lifted her tenderly onto the dining chair before putting the wheelchair aside and settling himself beside her. He made no fuss; it was over in a moment and accomplished with that gentleness so many giants possess. They were across the table from Beth, where she had placed herself as far away from him as possible. A tête-à-tête over dinner didn't suit her at all. She wanted to give herself as much space as possible while she tried to analyse her feelings. For the time being it was the small talk with him that she couldn't cope with. Later, when she'd been able to compose herself, she'd tell him she was troubled, and ask him straight out if she had reason to be.

A large round table seating ten people is not conducive to intimate conversation, and Beth was able to confine her remarks for the most part to Sally and Bob, who were sitting on either side of her. She realised she would have to face Ryan soon. There was no way he wouldn't seek her out, and if she avoided him she could well believe he would come pounding on her cabin door later. With Ryan not knowing that Juanita would be there it had all the potential for a very embarrassing situation.

' . . . don't you think?'

'I'm sorry, Sally, what did you say?'

'You're miles away, aren't you? I said, 'Wasn't it a fantastic tour today?' I can't wait for the next port of call.'

Beth agreed, managing to sound eager, though her thoughts were far from the pleasures in store. For the moment, though she'd never visited the places on the itinerary before, she couldn't summon up enthusiasm for the leaning tower of Pisa, the Roman remains, or indeed any of the treats awaiting them.

'Are you coming to this evening's lecture? I'm designated information gatherer. Bob much prefers to prop up the bar and be told what to admire when we get there, don't you, darling?' she said, leaning forward and speaking to her husband.

'Hmn? Yes, Sally, of course.'

Sally looked at Beth before casting her eyes to the ceiling. 'I don't think he even heard what I said. So, you'll be there?'

'Yes, yes, I will. I've heard he's a great speaker.'

In any other circumstances Beth would have been keen to go; but with her pleasure in the excursions now gone, she was just filling in time until her meeting with Ryan later.

★　★　★

'Why have you been avoiding me, Beth? What's wrong?'

Straight to the point — a sometimes uncomfortable characteristic, Beth was discovering. No blarney now; just confusion and pain in those beautiful brown eyes. They were standing on deck under the stars as the Mediterranean Sea welcomed them into her warm arms. They'd agreed the place hurriedly on the way from dinner to the lecture hall, but he'd sensed even then that she'd withdrawn from him.

Beth had no idea what to say. *How can I cross-examine him? It's hardly his fault I'm terrified because I've been betrayed. Look at his eyes. Those are not the eyes of a cheat.*

'It's nothing. I just had a blinding headache. It's going now. I'll be okay.' She could actually see the tension ease from those massive shoulders.

'I've been so worried, Mavourneen.'

'Mavourneen?'

'My darling. My sweetheart. It's Irish.' He smiled. She wasn't proof against his smile. Without even being invited she stepped into the circle of his arms. They spent a while reacquainting themselves with each other's lips until Ryan, with an urgency he couldn't disguise, broke away and said: 'I have to be alone with you, Beth. Properly alone.'

'It isn't as simple as that, Ryan.'

'Your cabin?'

'Now has another tenant. They told me when I took the job I'd have to share. Juanita came on board today, at Gibraltar.'

Ryan put the heel of his hand on his forehead, then ran fingers through his thick hair. 'I can't bear it. We have to find a way.'

With an urgency to match his, but a little more practicality, Beth struggled to think of one. 'One of the lifeboats. That's the only thing I can think of.'

'Of course. Tell me where, Beth.'

'I was joking, Ryan! I'm not creeping off to hide in a lifeboat. I have nothing to be ashamed of. Do you?' *There! I've managed to ask him the question without even meaning to.*

'Absolutely not! But I'm desperate for you, sweetheart. I need to be able to touch you, to feel you, to claim you.'

'Am I just a possession, then, for you to call your own?' But she was smiling.

'Possession? No, of course not. My own? I want nothing more than to make you my own. I've never . . . it's never . . . oh, Beth, I need you.'

The warm treacly sensation began again in the pit of her stomach.

'There's no way, Ryan. Not that I can think of. I want you, too; that's obvious I think. But until this cruise is over I just don't see how we can be together.'

'And when it's over I'll be going back to Dublin and you'll be . . . Where do you live, Beth?'

'Oxford. Just outside of Oxford.'

'I never realised a cruise could be this restricting. At least on dry land you can hire a hotel room.'

They could both see how ridiculous the situation was and both fortunately were blessed with a sense of humour. They started weaving the craziest plans to be alone together.

'It kind of kills the spontaneity a bit, doesn't it?' she asked him, smiling again, and he stilled, looking at her intently. He took her shoulders in his large hands and his eyes sparkled with passion.

'I don't think that's something we'll need to worry about, do you? Now, off to your cabin before I throw all caution to the wind. It's far too public here. Would you like me to walk you home?'

'It might be better if you stay here a while and cool off.'

'I love you, Beth. You know that, don't you? Even in this short time I love you.'

This is no deceiver. He wears his heart like a badge on his sleeve. 'I love you too, Ryan. Have done since the moment I saw you step onto this deck.'

7

The next port of call would be Toulon; and several of the passengers, Beth knew, were planning a visit to the opera house — the second largest in France, and a historic monument. With the ship remaining berthed until the following morning there was ample time for this scheduled excursion; but with a day at sea before they got there Beth was pretty busy.

Though her title was a bit of a misnomer as far as formal entertainment was concerned — those arrangements were all in place long before she'd even been offered the job — she was very much in demand during the day. At times it seemed that most of the 2,500 passengers wanted her simultaneously; and she loved it. She couldn't believe the variety of questions she was asked, from the price of a manicure to advice on which factor sun cream to use and several requests to apply it, though not from Ryan this time. Her work was keeping them apart and she was grateful for it. Doubts were at an end, but the strain of being together yet not being together was ameliorated by her having little opportunity to think about it.

When one of the passengers invited her to play golf with him Beth had as much fun as her partner. An American and travelling alone, he had been left widowed and had chosen cruising as a way of meeting people and not having to dine alone, a point several others had made to her. For singles as well as families she was discovering it was a great way to travel. He was a dedicated bridge player too. With that she couldn't help him but she gave him a run for his money on the putting green, discovering at the same time a talent she didn't know she possessed.

'Or it might just be beginner's luck,' she conceded.

'No, you played well. Perhaps you'll give me another game some time if we have the opportunity.'

'I'd love to, if only to find out if it was a fluke or not. Maybe I should take it up professionally?'

He laughed. 'Beth, I really do believe that's stretching it a bit too far. You're good — but not that good.'

*   *   *

There were a number of youngsters in or by the paddling pool, with a dedicated member of staff giving their parents the opportunity to relax in peace. Beth couldn't help thinking again how perfect an arrangement cruising was for so many people in so many different circumstances. Peace and quiet may have been the parents' lot, but they certainly weren't in evidence when she was dragged into the water by a couple of five-year-olds who insisted on finding out who could jump the highest and make the biggest

88

splash. Feeling a bit like a child herself, Beth joined in wholeheartedly.

'It's supposed to be for children only,' one of the helpers said, laughing at her.

'And I'm in my second childhood, so that includes me. What's your excuse?' she asked, her own laugh turning to a squeal as a boy with a somewhat mischievous grin threw a bucketful of water, drowning her curls. Undeterred, she picked up another bucket and chased him round the small pool. A water fight ensued in which there was no winner but a lot of happy boys and girls — and Beth.

★   ★   ★

Lunchtime found her changed out of her wet clothes and her hair dried into the butter-soft ringlets she'd hated as a child but was quite grateful for now. She didn't see Ryan and Siobhán in the buffet and assumed they were either having lunch by the pool or in one of the many other places on offer. Having eaten, she wandered through the inside areas and was surprised to find many people preferred the relaxation and quiet without venturing out into the sunshine. There was a rubber of bridge in progress; three people asleep in the library and one actually reading; and a number of players in the casino, where she understood they were likely to remain for much of the time, vacating only when the ship was in port and the casino closed. Oh, and Lydia and Ruth playing the inevitable game of Scrabble. They'd just finished and were about to begin another.

'Come and join us. We can play three-handed,' Ruth invited, so Beth did and was not the least bit surprised when she had to work hard to get anywhere near the scores they achieved.

'That was great fun. Can we do it again some time?'

'Certainly; perhaps you'll do better when you're not quite so focussed on your young man,' said Lydia. Oh dear.

That obvious, eh!

Beth went next to the spa, hoping to book a massage if there were any spare appointments in her time off. It was packed, as was the gym. Back on deck she allowed herself the luxury of spending a while with Ryan, who was sitting by the pool with his sister.

'I've missed you.' A simple statement, but he made her feel like the most precious thing in the world.

'You can see how much he appreciates my company, can't you?' Siobhán asked her directly. They both laughed and Ryan tried to look contrite, but didn't quite pull it off.

'Any chance I can see you later, Beth?'

'*A Midsummer Night's Dream* is on in the theatre this evening. I'll be there.'

'Then so will we be.'

★   ★   ★

'Do you have to sit through it twice — or even once?' Ryan asked Beth after he'd wheeled his sister's chair into place for the first performance.

'Probably not. There are enough members of staff to see that everyone's seated comfortably. Why?'

'Come with me.' It was a command, not a request.

'What are you talking about, Ryan? You can't just leave Siobhán sitting there on her own.'

'I can and I will. And so will you. It was her idea.'

'What!'

'I may just have mentioned our little problem to her. She's happy to sit through the play twice. She loves Shakespeare, and *The Dream* is her favourite. You're coming with me.'

She went meekly enough. It was what she wanted, too. He opened the door to reveal a room far larger and more luxurious than her own cabin. *So this is what it's like to be rich.* It was more like an apartment with a dedicated lounge area, the furniture covered inevitably in the company's cream and blue regalia.

92

On the small table was a bottle of champagne and two glasses. She smiled though she felt nervous, like a girl on her first date. 'You must have felt pretty sure of me.'

'No, not sure — but optimistic.' He grinned — definitely more a grin than a smile — and she responded as she felt she always would to this man. He took her hand almost ceremoniously and led her to the sofa. 'May I offer you a drink?' Ryan filled the glasses, handing one to her and sitting beside her. She found herself feeling grateful that he wasn't rushing her, though her need was as strong as his.

'We have four hours, Beth. Just four hours, but it's the beginning of a lifetime. To us and the future.'

'The future.'

They drank the toast. Put down the champagne flutes. His eyes were smouldering pools and she knew he was trembling; they both were.

Suddenly he stood, swept her up in his arms and carried her to the bed, laying her down gently. Ryan moved on to the bed beside her, leaning on one elbow to gaze again at this elfin girl who'd stolen his heart. In spite of his need he would not hurry. They would never have this moment again, this first time, and he wanted to make it perfect for her. Lying on his side, he cupped her face in his hands. Even at this slight touch her breathing quickened. For a moment they were suspended in time, till he moved to caress her neck with his lips, her body with his hands. She gasped and reached down to hold him but he caught her hand.

'Not yet or I'll never be able to wait.'

He held her wrists on the pillow on either side of her head and leaned towards her, kissed the corner of her mouth, her eyes, the curve of her chin. Beth felt Ryan's weight shift again as his hand grazed her waist, her hip.

'I need you to be naked,' he said, sounding hoarse as the words ripped from his throat; and somehow they removed the offending garments, his and hers. Skin touched burning skin as both were unable to control the demands of their own bodies, and then her hips rose to meet his as they reached their own heaven.

At long last they relaxed and lay side by side, staring at the ceiling.

'Ryan, this was so against the rules.'

'Some rules, Beth, are just made to be broken.'

She could hear the smile in his voice. She slept. He slept. They were holding hands.

* * *

Beth woke and brushed at the lobe of her ear, causing Ryan to protest as her hand caught his nose close to where he was nibbling. 'There's no romance in you, girl. Here I was, attempting to wake you gently on the chance that you might be prepared to go another round with me, and you brush me aside like a fly.'

'I thought you *were* a fly; and if you

think it's romantic to liken what we've just done to a boxing match then I want no more to do with you.' She smiled at him sleepily and with no small amount of affection.

'Just done! That was nearly two hours ago!'

The relief for them both was enormous, and now the initial desperation had been satisfied Beth was content to curl up in the protection of Ryan's arm and talk. Not so Ryan. Realising that ear nibbling wasn't doing the trick, he began gently to caress her body. The response was immediate and rewarding.

'Those are unfair tactics. How would you like it if I did that to you?'

'Yes please.'

Beth decided humouring him was the only sensible thing to do and cradled him gently in her hand — and suddenly for her, too, lying supported in the crook of his arm was no longer enough. Taking the initiative she explored him, teasing him until he moaned and lay back, giving himself up to this new ecstasy.

'You have to stop. Beth, you have to stop. *Now.*'

Realising that she'd brought him to the brink Beth stopped, only to find that Ryan was resuming his mapping of her own body. He knew. He knew exactly where to touch, exactly how much pressure to exert. How did he know?

'Ryan, please,' she wailed. Beth had never been so abandoned; had never known such a peak of excitement. 'Don't stop. Don't stop.'

As if he would. He brought her to a place she'd never been before, and after their second frantic union they collapsed, exhausted. Ryan looked at her with something approaching awe and spoke from his soul.

'Beth, it's been said that I have the Irish way with words, but suddenly I don't know what those words are. You've given me . . . what have you given me? A gift that cannot be described in any language I know. The last thing I expected to feel was humility. I thank you for your trust.'

Something had happened to them that evening, and neither would ever be the same again. Desperate to sleep, they nevertheless rose, showered and dressed quickly, and returned to the theatre where Siobhán was waiting.

8

The next few days passed in a haze of happiness for them both. While she couldn't go with Ryan and Siobhán on their planned excursions, Beth was content to fulfil her obligations to her job and snatch moments with him when she was able. They were always in public except for their nightly meetings on deck before parting, each to go to his or her own cabin.

Leaving Toulon behind, Beth spent a fabulous evening listening to Juanita's wonderful rendition of some of the popular arias she'd spoken of. The previous night's performance in Toulon, wonderful though it was, had been no better. The theatre was packed and the deep-throated voice brought a lump to her own and tears to her eyes. It was evident Beth wasn't the only one so moved, and she told Juanita later in their cabin how much she'd enjoyed her performance.

'It's easy to be good when you've been given a gift and love what you do. It's no credit to me that I was born with a voice. The credit is to those who taught me how to use it.'

'But to give pleasure to so many; that must be a great feeling.'

'You give pleasure too, Beth. Haven't you seen how people smile when you give them a helping hand, or just walk into a room?'

Beth asked about her family. There was a mother at home. No, no significant other. A seed germinated in Beth's head and she wondered if she'd be able to bring it to flower.

By the time the girls had finished talking the evening had advanced into night, and they both fell asleep contented with their lot. A day at sea was followed by a visit to Florence, where the choice was an expedition to Pisa or time in the city. Ryan and Siobhán had booked an excursion to the famous Tower and Beth went on the other trip, acting as aide to the guide. She was overwhelmed by their tour of the Uffizi Gallery, the interior of which was as magnificent as any external architecture she'd seen. She stood staring at Botticelli's 'Birth of Venus' for so long her group moved on without her — and she was supposed to be helping! How she wished Ryan had been able to share it with her. Her doubts over, she was now able to throw herself into the pleasure of being a tourist like any other.

The following day's scheduled stop was Rome, and as she had no obligations that day she joined Ryan and Siobhán. It was a full-on trip and every superlative used to describe Michelangelo's masterpiece couldn't do it justice, the splendour of the Sistine Chapel ceiling famed but the reality unimagined. Visiting the Colosseum too, it wasn't difficult to conjure up a vision of the contests between gladiators where so many had lost their lives;

to almost hear the roar of the ancient crowd, on their feet every one with their thumbs down. From there they walked to the Roman Forum, finally finishing the day at the Trevi Fountain. Inevitably they threw a coin; each had a wish.

'And yours was?'

'I'm not telling you that, Ryan. For one thing, if I do it won't come true. For another, I don't want to give you an inflated opinion of yourself, and that's the only clue you're getting.'

Siobhán laughed at them both and had her own secret wish.

* * *

'Fancy a nightcap, Juanita?' It was the end of a long day but Beth hadn't finished yet. 'It would be nice to wind down in the bar and listen to some gentle music.'

'That's a great idea. My feet are killing me but my head is still buzzing with all those wonderful things we saw today. I've been before many times but it's always a magical experience. I don't think I could sleep yet.'

They made their way to where Bruce, the resident pianist, was emulating Frank Sinatra, and doing it quite well too.

'I'd heard he was good but this is the first time I've actually seen him. The company runs so many different cruises our paths have never crossed before.'

'Let me introduce you, then. I got talking to him the day I came on board. Nice guy. Australian.' A fact that was obvious, of course, as soon as he spoke.

'Good to meet you, Juanita. I wanted to catch your show the other evening, but unfortunately I had to be here in the bar entertaining those who like their music a little less cultured.'

'Don't put yourself down. That last ballad you sang was beautiful.'

'Maybe we could do a duet? What do you say?'

'I'd love to. Are you really called Bruce or is it just a stage name?'

'I really am.'

Beth left them laughing and leafing through Bruce's material looking for something that would suit them both. She went to join Ryan and Siobhán where they were nursing a late night drink at one of the tables. She was well satisfied with her little attempt at matchmaking. It was up to them now. She didn't see Bruce look up at them and murmur to Juanita; didn't hear what he said.

'I'm surprised to see her with Ryan Donovan; surprised he's here at all.'

'I hope you and Bruce are going to play together for us one evening,' Beth said when she and Juanita met up later in their cabin. Juanita remained silent, her face solemn.

'What is it? What's the matter?'

'There's something I think you should know.'

'What can be so bad to make you look so serious?'

'It's about Ryan.'

'What? What is about Ryan?'

'I don't know how to tell you.'

'Tell me straight, whatever it is. Come on, Juanita, tell me,' Beth, the fear hitting her again with full force, almost screamed at her.

'Back in Ireland, when Siobhán had her accident, well it appears it may not have been an accident.'

'What are you saying?'

'Apparently Ryan and Niall — Siobhán's husband, you know — didn't get on; no, it was stronger than that. A Protestant and a Catholic. Even I understand how bad these things can be. There is some suspicion the car's brakes were tampered with. There's an investigation in progress. It seems Ryan may have . . . ' She left the sentence unfinished. It wasn't difficult for Beth to fill the gap.

'I don't believe it! How do you know? Who told you?'

'Bruce said it was in the news the last time he did a UK cruise. Dublin was one of the ports of call. There'd been a car crash. Siobhán's husband and daughter were killed and she lost the baby she was expecting. That's how she ended up in a wheelchair.'

'And they suspect Ryan of tampering with the car? Outrageous!'

'I agree. But once it was suggested — anonymously, Bruce said; and of course Ryan's name wasn't mentioned, but he was certainly alluded to — the Garda had to look into it. Presumably they haven't found anything to implicate him or Ryan wouldn't be here. It certainly isn't resolved yet. As soon as Bruce saw him on board he Googled to find out.'

Beth sank onto the bed, a ghastly white accentuated by the cream duvet cover.

'There's nothing conclusive yet,' Juanita said. 'They wouldn't have allowed Ryan to travel if they'd had anything against him. I didn't know what to do but I thought you should know. I don't want to see you hurt, Beth.'

Too late. Far far too late. Beth went

to bed and cried as if her heart was breaking, which indeed it was.

★ ★ ★

The following day was a carefree one for the Donovans, Ryan's sister laughing at his attempts to play golf where he'd demonstrated a complete lack of ability or feel for the game. The only immediate blot on his landscape was his inability to tell Beth what lay behind him — and what possibly lay in front. He wanted so much to confide in her; had almost done so the night before they'd docked in Gibraltar. She'd told him all about Gerry and he was just going to launch into a confession — no, not that; he wasn't guilty of anything other than withholding information from Beth — but something held him back and the moment passed. He was blissfully unaware of her conversation with Juanita the night before and had enjoyed the day with an easy mind, looking forward to seeing her again in the evening, on deck if no other opportunity presented itself.

To say that Beth's heart was troubled was a huge understatement. Already vulnerable after her experience with Gerry, the news she'd heard was like kicking a puppy while it was down. *Am I in love with a murderer? Could this giant of a man, so gentle with me, so tender, have committed such a terrible crime?* She couldn't believe it. She wouldn't believe it. Beth went to confront Bruce.

'As far as I understood it at the time, initially there had been no thought of anything but a tragic accident. But Ryan and his brother-in-law didn't get on, no doubt about that. No, it was more than that. In a country where feelings run so deep, the relationship between two men with such opposing views who lived in such close proximity must have been like a time bomb waiting to explode. Then there was an anonymous phone call. Ryan's name wasn't mentioned, evidently, but it's easy enough to point a finger without, isn't it?'

'But that doesn't make Ryan capable of murder.'

'I've told you everything I know, Beth. I wish there was more.'

Her mind in turmoil, Beth's instinct was to hide in her cabin but she was made of sterner stuff. *Anyway, I've done enough sobbing over Gerry and weeping in the privacy of my room isn't going to benefit me at all. I'm going to meet this face-on.* Somehow the thought didn't give her any comfort at all.

★   ★   ★

At approximately the same time Siobhán was watching Ryan playing golf, Beth came to a firm and irrevocable decision. Desperate though she was to believe the rumour about Ryan would be disproved, it seemed the odds were stacked against him. It didn't take much in that troubled country for sores to be opened, for wounds to be laid bare. Ryan and Niall hadn't got on — so much was obvious — but premeditated murder! Even a crime of passion would be better than that.

The most damning thing as far as Beth was concerned, though, was that Ryan hadn't told her himself. It would have made all the difference but if he could keep something so huge from her now how did that bode for their future. They'd known each other for only a week now but so intimately, and not just on a physical level. It had felt like a meeting of minds, only it seemed one of those minds was holding something back. He'd talked of a future with her. How could he not have told her of the past, of this other possible future? She just couldn't bear the prospect of being with him for the months or maybe years it would take to resolve the situation, only to have it culminate in his conviction. Much as she loved him — and she was absolutely sure that she loved him, even after so little time: *I just do! The amount of time is irrelevant* — her already wounded heart wouldn't recover if the nagging fear turned into a monstrous reality. Her only choice was to cut and run — not that there was anywhere at the moment she could run to. Feeling as if she were going to attend a funeral rather than a sociable meal, Beth went to the dining room.

'What is it, Beth? What's wrong?'

There was never any preamble with this man. If he had something to say he'd say it — *except for the one thing he should have told me and didn't,* Beth thought bitterly. They were standing in their usual place on deck and she was trying to summon all her resources; heaven knew she was going to need them. *He knows there's something badly wrong. I have to tell him right out. Look at him. Ther's no blarney now; just confusion and pain in those beautiful brown eyes.* She would be direct too. She owed him that much; at least that much. It didn't make it any easier though. Between making her decision and deciding on her strategy, she realised that nothing short of brutality would persuade him to let her go.

'I've had a call from Gerry. He's left his wife, Ryan. He wants me back.'

Ryan looked stunned; almost reeled under the blow. She felt as if there was a rock in the place where her heart should be. She knew he loved her; knew that she had to be this cruel. If she'd given him any sort of an opening he would have taken it. She didn't think she'd be able to maintain the lie, so hard to tell in the first place, if he fought back; so she gave him no opening.

'And what did you tell him?'

'He said he didn't realise how much I meant to him until I'd gone; that he couldn't live without me.'

This is unbearable. How can I do this — twist the knife? How can I inflict so much hurt on the man I love?

'And what did you tell him?' he repeated.

'I said we'd give it another try.'

'And us, Beth. What about us?'

'I'm so sorry, Ryan. There can't be any us. I don't know how it happened. Being on the rebound . . . the romance of a cruise . . . I don't know. I didn't mean to hurt you. But it isn't real. How could it be after so short a time?' *But it is, and I knew it the moment I saw you.*

'Nothing in my life before has ever been more real, Beth. I thought it was the same for you.'

'I was wrong. I realised when Gerry called that this was just a fantasy. I'm so sorry, Ryan.'

She saw disbelief, then doubt and finally acceptance and she watched as the sparkle disappeared before the veil came down over his eyes. All this she could see clearly in the moonlight. She knew she'd lost him now, forever; and all she could remember was Siobhán, sitting by the pool saying, 'Be kind to him, Beth. He's been through a lot.' And her reply: 'I hope to make it my life's work, being kind to him.'

9

The following day was spent without docking anywhere, and Beth had never felt more at sea than she did then. Because there was no port of call there were more demands on her time, and she could only be grateful. The sun that poured down on them was in sharp contrast to the coldness in her heart. Outwardly she was the epitome of smiling efficiency, a hostess doing her job to perfection. The passengers were not to know that she was working almost entirely on automatic while she spent most of the day internalising. Bruce's words kept coming back to her. 'Ryan and his brother-in-law didn't get on, no doubt about that.' Was it really so damning? Didn't lots of young men like to push their weight around? Wasn't it just part of growing up? Maybe growing up in Ireland where feelings ran so high moved everything up a notch or two.

But I didn't even ask him. It's like I've condemned him out of hand.

Yes, but it doesn't alter the fact that he's under suspicion for murder.

No, but I've condemned him for that too, haven't I — without a hearing.

Beth saw Ryan twice during her rounds; once she moved away before he'd noticed her, the second time he turned and walked off as she approached the pool area. He left Siobhán lying on the sunbed and Beth took her courage in both hands and went over to her. She came straight to the point.

'How is he?' No small talk. This was too important. Neither of them could make polite conversation under the circumstances.

'Not good. What happened, Beth?'

'I can't talk about it. I'm sorry.'

'He told me you were sorry. It hasn't made him feel any better.' There was no sarcasm in her voice; just a flat statement. 'Look, if there's anything I can do . . . '

A quick shake of the head was all Beth could give in reply, but in her eyes Siobhán saw the same despair she'd seen in her brother's. Whatever it was that had compelled Beth to cut the tie between her and Ryan, it wasn't because she didn't love him anymore. Siobhán wished she knew what had been said during that fateful discussion but neither party was confiding in her, and without being in possession of the facts there was nothing she could do to help.

Another passenger waved at Beth, calling her name, and Siobhán watched as the mask slid into place and the *Mediterranean Adventurer*'s hostess moved on to do her job. Almost as soon as she'd gone Ryan returned. Had he been watching them? Siobhán wondered. Probably. Did he ask what had happened? No, he just carried on as if the whole incident hadn't taken place. She rather thought the pair of them needed their heads banging together.

* * *

A once-famous but now slightly ageing comedian was scheduled for the evening's entertainment. Was the cruise line cutting corners? Not a bit of it. Beth had never been to one of his shows before but like most comics she knew, his stand-up performance went far beyond what was permitted on the television — except on a ship where there were children in the audience and the possibility that he could cause offence. Consequently Desmond had adapted his script to fit the circumstances.

As before, Beth waited at the entrance to greet the passengers before they found their way to the armchair-like seats. She looked in vain for the Donovans, wanting them to be there but grateful when they didn't show. In spite of her misery she found herself smiling from time to time, even laughing out loud at one particularly funny sketch. Desmond delighted his public, calling some of them on to the stage, children and adults alike. Whether it was the sea air or the relaxation of being on holiday nobody knew, but there were several who found their previous inhibitions left behind as they threw themselves wholeheartedly into the show. Desmond had lost none of his skill or talent with his advancing years and he left his audience wanting more, as any good professional performer should.

When the second production was due to begin Beth looked again for Siobhán and Ryan but once more they were, to her at least, conspicuous by their absence. *They haven't changed their sitting in the dining room then. I bet he won't be waiting for me with a meal this time*, she thought, remembering how he'd teased her about dribbling.

She was grateful to accept the

comedian's escort to the bar at the end of the show because 'It's thirsty work up there and I never allow myself a wee dram beforehand. Would you care to join me?' They both ordered a sandwich and a couple of singers from the Musical Extravaganza joined them for a nightcap. Beth was delighted to see Juanita draped over the piano talking to Bruce in between songs. It looked like things were going well there. At the same time, though, it reminded her of her own loss. If anyone noticed that Beth appeared distracted or that her eyes kept darting up every time anyone came into the room, they were polite enough not to mention it.

'My wife never comes to watch me at these events,' Desmond was saying. 'I suppose over the years she's seen enough and heard all my jokes a hundred times. She prefers to spend her evening in the casino. They're usually good on board and this one's no different from the rest.'

'I didn't realise your wife was with you.'

'Every time, Beth. It's a paid holiday for us really; I don't work every night and because it's a one man show I don't even need much rehearsal time. The pianist has my musical introduction and there really isn't much more to it than that. No, it's a great life. I used to think Roma might get bored but she never has. She's as eager as I am whenever the opportunity comes up.'

'You do this a lot?'

'Whenever I can. Don't you?'

'First time.' And the last, she thought. *I'll never be able to do this again without thinking about what might have been.*

'Well, I'm off to the casino to fetch Roma. It's time for bed. Do you want to come with me? I'm sure she'd like to meet you.'

'I'd love to. I might even have a flutter myself. I only had a quick look in when I was trying to take on board the ship's layout. It's like a small town, isn't it, the ship I mean?

'Yes, and if you take a wrong turning you might find a real treasure hidden away in a back street. Here we are then. After you.' He stood back at the entrance to let her go in front of him. That was when Beth saw Ryan.

He was sitting at the roulette table. There was no sign of Siobhán and Beth could only assume she'd already gone to bed. Even in these few days it hadn't escaped her notice that late nights were not on Siobhán's agenda. Beth had no idea if she was in pain, or on medication that tired her out, followed by the thought that she probably never would know now. Aside from her feelings for Ryan, this was cause for some regret. Though it was too soon for a strong bond to have formed there was nevertheless an affinity between the two young women which both, given the opportunity, would have chosen to explore. For Beth it just added to her loss.

Desmond collected a reluctant Roma

from the blackjack table and introduced her to Beth. 'Why does he always come to get me when I've started on a winning streak? It's like he knows I've just begun to enjoy myself,' she said, but she was smiling. 'I've seen a very pretty necklace in the ship's shop that I was going to get with my winnings. Des, you'll just have to buy it for me yourself. Beth, it's been lovely meeting you but I'm off now for some beauty sleep. Goodnight.' Roma yawned her way out of the casino.

Beth, after exchanging money for chips, sat down at a one-armed bandit, keeping Ryan within view while making sure he didn't know she was there. She wondered if he'd been hiding there all evening and if it hurt him as much to see her as it did her every time she looked at him. She watched him in profile, studying him, trying to remember every treasured detail of his face: the strength of his jaw, the muscle that worked in his cheek. She wanted so much to go to his side; to share his excitement if he won or commiserate as the croupier cleared the table.

She saw him throw back his drink, Irish whiskey maybe, in one gulp and order another. A man of his stature almost certainly had a large capacity for alcohol, but he didn't look as if he was carrying it well and she wondered how much he'd had. She questioned whether it was possible to drown one's sorrows and even considered it for a fleeting moment before rejecting the idea. *I need all my wits about me, both for work and in defence of my sanity. If I weaken I'll just beg him to take me back.* There was the question of pride of course. Having made her decision, Beth would stick with it. She had her name to live up to after all.

As the evening advanced into night people began drifting away, but the figure at the wheel turned his head only to order another drink. From where she sat she couldn't see if he was winning or losing, but she knew it would make no difference either way. He was going through the motions, knowing that even if he went to bed wakefulness would be his companion. She knew because there was no way she would be able to sleep herself.

Eventually, though, she stood up and taking her sadness with her went to her cabin. Juanita wasn't back yet. Beth was grateful. She looked in the mirror as she cleaned her teeth, noticing the dark shadows under her eyes. Perched on the washstand was a picture of her and Ryan taken at the captain's reception on the first night. They looked so happy, both of them. She'd posed with all the passengers. This was the only photo she'd kept. It was all she had of him now.

*   *   *

The next port of call was Seville. Beth didn't even bother to disembark. She was carrying her heartbreak over Ryan on the back of being betrayed by Gerry and had no inclination to view the sights. Vulnerable before she met Ryan but so determined to be the mistress of her own salvation, she'd been floored almost immediately, the helter-skelter of her life causing her stomach to lurch as if she were riding the real thing, but there was worse to come.

The one thing she'd been so sure of was Ryan's love for her. They'd split because of her actions, not his. The shock then, when it came, was greater than she could have imagined. She saw him arm in arm with Allegra, the lovely Italian, at the Donovans' table. She'd sat at his right hand every mealtime but Beth had been secure enough not to see the dark-haired beauty as a rival. She'd noticed Ryan flirting with Allegra, but then Ryan flirted with everyone; it was who he was and he was completely unaware of doing it — except when he intended to, and then he really was a force to be reckoned with.

They were walking on the deck before dinner and Siobhán was nowhere to be seen. It was pure accident that Beth was even there but she'd felt the need for a bit of fresh air, though it was sucked from her body when she saw the two together. Ryan, looking down at the fiery young woman, was patting her hand where it rested on his arm. Beth could see the passion in her face though Ryan himself was half-turned away and his features hidden from view. *Well that didn't take him long, did it? It seems he's managed to find consolation fairly quickly.* Tears streaming down her cheeks, Beth doubled back. She didn't see Ryan take Allegra by the shoulders; didn't watch as he moved back a step; didn't hear as he told Allegra — in the gentlest possible way — that he wasn't a free man.

'What a shame. With your hair and colouring and my hair and colouring we would have made a stunning couple.'

Ryan smiled at her, happy that she had taken rejection so well; but then her heart wasn't engaged as his had been when rejection came to him. A light

126

flirtation was all she wanted, and now that they had established their boundaries both were content to enjoy each other's company for the duration of the cruise. Consequently, the next time Beth saw Ryan, it was when he was wheeling Siobhán down the gangway with Allegra at his side, all three of them determined to make the most of what Lisbon, next on the agenda, had to offer in the time available to them.

* * *

Beth spent much of the rest of the cruise dividing her time equally between avoiding Ryan and trying to catch a glimpse of this personification of her dreams. It didn't take her long to discover that Allegra joined Ryan and his sister every night for the evening's entertainment. She knew also that after Siobhán had gone to bed Ryan would spend hours alone in the casino. It was some small consolation that at least he hadn't jumped straight from her bed into someone else's. Beth didn't follow every night to watch him gambling; didn't know that he sat whiskey at his right hand and a pile of chips in front of him that increased or diminished with the luck of the spin; didn't know that the whole procedure seemed to make little difference to the lonely figure at the roulette table. Unable to stop herself, there were times when she would take her place at one of the 'bandits', hidden from his view, though this was almost an irrelevance as he rarely lifted his eyes from the table or turned his head away, other than to order another drink or to replenish his stock of chips if he was on a losing streak. It wasn't for her to know the minutes or hours at the table were all the same to him. A filler; a plaster too small to cover his gaping wound.

Her own turmoil wasn't unlike his. *Why am I torturing myself like this?* But even as she asked herself the question she knew the answer. Another few days and she'd never see him again. She was trying to remember every precious detail, like a computer committing data to its memory bank, only she had no external hard disc on which to back up her images. Her unreliable human memory would be all she would have. The visit to Rome, her wish at the Trevi Fountain, seemed unreal now and would certainly not be fulfilled. *What is the matter with me? I made the choice and I must accept the consequences.*

Vigo, and one last day at sea, and all too soon they reached their final destination. Though she'd tried hard to prepare herself for the moment, Beth felt bereft as members of Captain Roberts's crew secured the *Mediterranean Adventurer* to the dock in Southampton harbour. Beth had watched as the passengers disembarked; seen Ryan wheeling Siobhán from the ship. He'd turned for one last look — seeking her out, she knew — but her courage failed her and she'd stepped back into the shadows. She told herself it was kinder that way, but in truth there was no kind way. She'd inflicted a bitter wound on the person she cared for most in the whole world, on a whim, on the basis of something that might never happen because someone else had destroyed her trust. She'd watched as he turned away and walked out of her life forever.

10

In spite of removing every single one of Gerry's possessions, there were reminders of him everywhere in Beth's flat: the skew-whiff footstool, the funny mug he'd bought her last Christmas, the wine stain. She remembered the incident so clearly, even now.

'It was an accident, Beth. I'm so sorry.'

Beth had tried hard not to cry.

'We'll get a new carpet,' he'd promised when no amount of cleaning removed the offending stain.

She didn't want a new carpet. Beth had spent ages finding just the right one — something Gerry would never be able to understand. 'Surely a cream carpet is a cream carpet?' he'd asked her.

She knew she wouldn't be able to stay there now. The flat that she'd chosen and equipped with so much love had become a torture chamber. She put it up for rent as soon as she got back to Oxford. It had been snapped up immediately and the new tenants were going to move in at the beginning of the month. Beth didn't search for a new home; home is where the heart is and to her certain knowledge hers was in Dublin. Simon and Linda, her boss and his wife, offered her the granny annexe attached to their house until she could find a place to rent; an open-ended offer, they said.

'We're hoping it will be a long while before we'll need it. It'll be for our parents eventually, but in the meantime we rent it out and the last tenant vacated recently, so it's free if you want it.'

'I love it, Simon, but I can see the rent's going to be more than my flat will realise.'

'I shouldn't think there'd be too much of a discrepancy. Why don't you move in, for the time being if you like?

It will suit us to have it occupied and leave you free to look for what you want without pressure.'

Beth insisted on paying the going rate. 'I can afford the extra. My boss and his wife pay me an exorbitant salary.'

'Yeah, I hear they're great people.'

'I may have to ask for a tiny increase though.'

Simon laughed. 'In your dreams.'

★ ★ ★

She moved in immediately, not able to face going back to the flat that now held only painful memories. Her pain moved with her. Beth picked her job back up quickly enough, but couldn't do the same for the pieces of her broken heart.

'We've missed you, Beth. Simon's certainly missed you. He likes to think it's him who runs the business, but nobody's in any doubt about the value of your contribution. Where your job is concerned he doesn't have a clue.'

Beth didn't suffer from undue modesty regarding her profession but it was good to have Linda's approbation. She was aware of her own worth as far as her job was concerned. It was only in her love life that she was lacking. Well, instead of just a career it would now be her life's work. She had nothing else. *And whose fault is that? I held happiness in the palm of my hand and threw it away.*

Beth was to have many internalised conversations like this one, none satisfactory, and none less so than when Simon gave her yet another day off to pack the few things she was taking with her. As for the rest, she had no use for them now. She turned her back on them and hoped her tenant wouldn't find the wine stain as offensive as she did. The most precious thing she owned she'd brought home with her from the *Mediterranean Adventurer*. Otherwise there was little she wanted; little she wanted reminding of. *It's not like I'm making a home for anyone. Not likely to either.* Beth turned the key in the lock for the last time, dropped it into the managing agents and went to her new home.

★ ★ ★

The next few weeks were the longest and loneliest Beth had ever spent. The demands of her job were considerable, and time should have flown, but it didn't. She felt miserable. She felt awful. She was permanently tired. Her face looked pale underneath her rapidly fading tan. There were other things going on as well and things were not going on too that should have been. Then she began throwing up. Finally, but with little doubt in her mind, Beth made an appointment to see the doctor.

'It's quite normal to feel like this. Try and take it easy and put your feet up when you can but there's no need to coddle yourself. Your blood pressure's fine. You're a healthy young woman; you should sail through this.'

'But I'm on the pill! How can I be pregnant?'

'Well, sometimes some of the little blighters get through.' He looked at Beth's notes. 'It seems I prescribed an antibiotic for a throat infection a few days before you went away. That can sometimes interfere with the efficacy of a contraceptive.'

'Oh. I see.'

'Anyway, have a word with one of the receptionists on your way out. She'll arrange for you to see the midwife and begin your antenatal care.'

'Thank you, Doctor.' An automatic response, but was she really thankful? Nothing had prepared her for this. She was carrying a baby; Ryan's baby. Hope fluttered in her breast, but it fluttered and died. She couldn't tell him. For all the same reasons she'd lied about leaving him, she couldn't tell him. If things went against Ryan, her baby would be the child of a convicted murderer. Keeping Ryan's identity secret meant it wouldn't have to live with such awful knowledge. She had to ask herself, though, what if his name was cleared? *But what if it isn't? How can I keep a child from its father? How can I keep a father from his child? Oh, God help me, I don't know what to do.*

Beth knew deep down that she ought to tell Ryan. How could she be so cruel as to keep the baby from him, and from the aunt who had lost her own children? She was a conscientious young woman with strong principles, but she had someone else to think about now; someone who was helpless and would need her to do the right thing. *But what is the right thing? I have to protect my child.* There was no other right thing. *A child without a father isn't so unusual. There are many single parent families. Many single mothers. It's not remarkable anymore. There aren't too many children, though, whose parent has been found guilty of taking another man's life. Now that would be remarkable.* Beth kept going round in circles pitting one argument against another, satisfied with none of the conclusions but sticking still to her decision because of the baby.

Back in the office Beth went to tell Simon the good news.

'That's great, Beth. I'm so pleased for you. You needn't think it means I'm going to let you go though. We can sort out maternity leave; keep your job open for you. You can even work from home some of the time if you need to; most of the time in fact. You can still do all the co-ordinating, even if we have to find someone else to be on site at the events. Don't worry, Beth. We'll look after you, if this is what you want.'

If this is what I want? What about an abortion? It had never occurred to her and she dismissed the thought immediately. She wanted this baby. She would keep this baby. It was all she would have of Ryan, more than she'd ever dreamed of, far more than she had any right to expect. Or, in her own opinion, than she deserved.

'Hi, Mum. Just thought I'd give you a quick call. How are you? You okay?'

'I'm fine. We both are. You?'

'Yes, me too. Are you home on Saturday? I thought I'd come visit.'

'That would be lovely. It's been ages since we've seen you. Do you want lunch? Supper?'

'No thanks, Mum. Tea will be fine. See you then.'

Beth clicked off, relieved the first hurdle at least was over. If the phone call was that much of an ordeal how was it going to be when she actually saw them face to face; broke the news? Truth to tell, she wasn't sure how they would take it. They were both so proud of her, of how much she'd achieved. She knew they'd been pleased at her split with Gerry; they'd never thought he was worthy of her. Looked like they were right.

'You can move on now, Beth. You know I didn't think he was the right man for you.'

'What father ever thinks anyone is good enough for their daughter?' she'd teased him.

'That's true enough, I suspect. Let's hope you do better with the next one. All Mum and I want is for you to be happy.'

And that was also true enough, but would they see this as being the path to her happiness? As she'd grown accustomed to her pregnancy, Beth had come to realise just how lucky she was. She'd had her ups and downs, particularly her downs, but she hadn't behaved impeccably either. Look what she was doing now, keeping a baby from its father. How blessed she was that she would always have a part of Ryan to remember him by, to be a constant reminder of what might have been. She couldn't believe him capable of murder, but what if he had done this awful thing? Is fiddling with the brakes, or whatever, any less of a crime because he hadn't stood in front of a man and pulled the trigger? Had he known his pregnant sister and niece would be in the car? No! No! No! He'd known none of it because he wasn't guilty. But what if — ?

'Hello, Mum, Dad. It's great to see you.'

'Come in, girl. You look worn out. Simon been pushing you to make up for lost time, has he?'

'No Dad, of course he hasn't.'

'Well sit down with your mother while I make a cup of tea.'

'Thanks, Dad.'

'You look like you're bursting. Is there something you want to tell us, Beth?'

What was it with mothers? Were they all omniscient or was it just hers?

'Yes, Mum, there is. Can we wait till Dad comes in? This is something you both need to hear.'

Her parents sat side by side on the sofa opposite her, waiting anxiously for whatever it was she had to tell them; their only daughter, their only child.

'I'm pregnant. Ten weeks now. No,

it's not showing yet.' She smiled briefly as her mother's gaze dropped from her face to her tummy. 'But it's definite. I'm having a baby.'

'I'll kill that blighter when I get hold of him.'

'It's not Gerry's, Dad. It's someone I met on the ship. Gerry and I were already over.'

'And you jumped straight into bed with another man?'

Beth could hear the bewilderment and anger in her father's voice. She didn't blame him. He was right after all. She looked at her mother.

'Who is he, Beth? When can we meet him?'

'You can't, Mum. I'm not with him anymore and I'm not going to be. I'm having this baby on my own. He doesn't know and he isn't going to know.'

'You haven't told him?'

It sounded like an accusation. Perhaps it was.

'No, Mum. What would be the point?

Like I said, we're not together now.'

'But a father has a right to know.'

Since Beth had had this same argument with herself many times recently, it didn't help to have it repeated by her mother.

'There's no point.'

Something in Beth's tone told her parents it would be futile to press her further, but she could see the disapproval and the disappointment in her father's face.

'Do you want to come home? Move back in with us? You know we'd love to have you, both of you.'

'No Mum, thank you. It's a wonderful offer and no more than I'd expect from the best parents in the world, but I want to keep my job. There are all sorts of ways I can have the baby and carry on working, and it would be much too far to commute from here.'

She knew it would be difficult for them to understand. They were brought up in an age where a mother stayed at home with her child if possible. They were making it possible and she was rejecting them.

'You're going to put your baby into care?'

'No, of course I'm not. A lot of what I do can be done from home, but I do need to carry on working.'

'Well, whatever we can do you know you only have to ask.'

Beth was more surprised by what her mother didn't say than what she did. There were no more recriminations. Her mother sensed there was more here than met the eye, but she realised she would only find out if and when Beth was ready to tell her. One thing Beth was sure about: her mother must never know who the father was. If she knew Ryan's identity, and how Beth felt about him, she'd cross to the other side of the world if need be for the sake of her daughter.

11

Four months in and thank goodness the nausea had stopped. Beth arranged to meet Claire for lunch one Saturday. She found for the first time in her pregnancy that she was absolutely ravenous.

'Why are you laughing? Have I got cream on my nose or something?' Beth asked.

'I have never seen you eat so much. I'm not sure I've ever seen anyone eat that much.'

'I'm making up for lost time. Lately I've been ejecting more than I've eaten; so much so that I actually lost weight. I even told the midwife, I was so worried.'

'And she said?'

'Don't worry,' whereupon both girls collapsed giggling and Beth ended up clutching her tummy where the evidence of her impending motherhood was by now clearly visible.

'I must say you look fantastic. It obviously suits you.'

'Yeah, I feel great now.'

'Now?'

'Now I've stopped heaving. Now that Mum and Dad have accepted there isn't going to be another half. Now that I'm nearly halfway through and can start making plans.'

'Plans?'

'Whether or not to work from home some of the time. I'd rather not. I'm far better with people around. How soon I can go back to work after the baby. Simon said it'd be okay for me to take the baby with me. Well, you know him. It's that sort of a company. No rigid rules or standing on ceremony. They've been great, you know; him and Linda. She's even talking about hands-on help. They can't have any of their own, and work is more of a hobby than a job for her. She's got plenty of free time if she wants it.'

'Lucky you.'

'You know I really think I am, in spite of everything.'

'You're not pissed off with me then, for taking my place on the cruise?'

Beth looked at her friend over the one cup of coffee she allowed herself a day. Even when she'd been feeling rough she'd still missed the coffee.

'I don't know how to explain, Claire. If someone had asked me before I'd have said no way; but I've had an experience some people never have the whole of their lives. How can I be sorry for that? I'll never see Ryan again but what we shared was something so special I can't even begin to describe it. If I try it just diminishes it somehow. And now I'm going to have something, just as special in its own way, in recognition of what we had. No, that sounds all wrong but . . . '

'You don't have to explain, Beth. Just as long as you're happy.'

'You have no idea how much it helps to be able to talk to you. There's not another soul who knows who the father is; no one else I can tell.'

Beth had confided in Claire almost as soon as she'd known herself. The relief of being able to share with someone had helped immensely.

'What do you think?' Beth knew it was an unfair question even as she asked it but the reply came back with no hesitation from Claire.

'That you're far better off on your own than you would have been if you'd ended up being with that two-timing boyfriend you had before. And in any case you're not going to be on your own. You're going to have a baby.'

'I know. I can still hardly believe it.'

'Like I said, as long as you're happy. Fancy another crème brûlée?'

* * *

Ryan left the ship if not a broken man then certainly a battered and bewildered one. After the darkest period of his life he thought he had found happiness, only to discover that there were even more profound depths into which he had been flung. How could he have been so wrong? For the shortest of times he'd believed he was the luckiest man on earth, that he would be able to cope with all of the difficulties he knew were to come. With Beth at his side he could survive it all. In a few moments she had shattered his romantic illusions. What was it she'd said? 'Being on the rebound . . . the romance of a cruise . . . I don't know. But it isn't real.' It had been real enough to him; real enough to prepare him to face his accusers. Now he had nothing, less than nothing; but still he had to be strong for Siobhán.

'What happened, Ryan? What did she say?'

'That it was a shipboard romance.' She could almost hear him grinding his teeth. 'That she was sorry. Sorry!'

Siobhán looked at the despair in her brother's eyes. She'd seen her own happiness disappear in a moment and knew the feeling of emptiness, the vacuum where her heart used to be. All this she saw in Ryan's face.

'Not to worry, girl. We'll get through this. The most important thing now is for you to get better. We both have a lot in front of us.'

The journey from Dublin to Southampton two weeks before hadn't been one of unadulterated excitement, they'd been through too much for that, but at least their spirits had lifted as soon as they'd got on board. They'd been prepared to make as much of it as they could, for the sake of Siobhán's health and to try, not to forget but at least to ease the pain. The return trip was as solemn as the day they'd buried her husband and daughter.

They stayed overnight in Liverpool on the way home, just as they had before. They ate in silence — no need now to act in front of the others; no need for Ryan to pretend he was having a great time. He'd been good at it, those last days of the cruise, drawing on his Irish blarney that had so deserted him the night he'd spent with Beth. Allegra had helped him too. She'd had no illusions and just wanted to enjoy the company of a gorgeous man; it was much more fun than spending time in between meals on her own. Neither had touched the other emotionally and it helped Ryan to maintain a front when he was in public. Only when Siobhán was in bed had he let the mask drop, allowed himself the luxury of drinking himself to oblivion. It hadn't worked. He found out it was all a big lie — sorrows don't drown in alcohol. If anything they become heightened.

His world was out of kilter. The night he'd spent with Beth, that was his only reality. It was a night he'd never forget. It was as if all the rest was fiction. And now he was on his way back to Dublin to await his fate. Did he care? Not much, except for Siobhán; his brave funny sister whose own loss had been so great and who even now was wondering if she'd ever walk again. Catching the ferry early in the morning they had time to reflect this was no cruise ship. Even the weather turned against them and they drove home in grey drizzle, tired and worn out.

'Well that just about matches me mood, eh, sis?'

Ryan made a stab at light irony but Siobhán couldn't even summon a smile. When they reached home he prepared them a simple meal they both could have done without and which in fact they hardly touched. He carried Siobhán up the stairs to bed then he went into Caitlan's room, the room where he'd stayed ever since the accident. He closed the door.

★　★　★

For Siobhán the round of physiotherapy that had started after the accident began all over again. A session every other day with an occupational therapist and in between exercises for those parts of her body she was able to move unaided. She could see the logic of the latter but most definitely not secondary discipline. Terrified that the rest of her would atrophy and become as useless as her legs, she was absolutely diligent about maintaining the regime that had been put in place for her. Harder were the hours spent watching someone massaging her lower limbs, seemingly to no avail.

'Sure it'll be okay, darlin'. You've just got to give it time,' said one of her army of helpers when she was found sobbing one morning after Ryan had gone to work. Siobhán was beginning to lose faith in ever being able to walk again, no matter how many times they reassured her, no matter how often the doctor told her she had to be patient.

'You were pinioned in your seat for that long before they cut you free, but I am absolutely convinced it will all come back, the feeling first and then the movement,' he'd said the last time she'd seen him. So far though there'd been nothing. No sensation; no reflex action; just an inability to gain any mastery over her own limbs.

'Why are you doubting, Siobhán, when they're so adamant you're going to get better?'

'Because it's taking so long, Ryan. It's been months now. I don't feel anything; not even if you stick a pin in me. Go on, try it. Stick a pin in me.'

'Don't be silly.'

'No, I mean it. Then you'll see why I don't believe them.'

Ryan took a pin and winced as he thought how it would feel if anyone plunged it into his own flesh. Siobhán wasn't to be deterred.

'Come on, Ryan. Do it. Do it!'

Ryan did it. He plunged the needle into her leg.

'Oh my God, oh my God, oh my God. I can feel it. Quick; try the other one.'

No reaction from the other leg, but it was a beginning. If one had begun surely the other would follow. From that day onwards Siobhán doubled her efforts. She was given new exercises it was hoped would accelerate the improvement in her left leg. A week later sensation returned to her right.

'If you'd have asked me a year ago would I pleased if someone stuck a pin in my leg I'd have laughed at them. It doesn't hurt yet, I'm glad to say. The feeling is almost like a butterfly crawling on my skin, but it's there. Gentle, tender almost, and definitely there. It won't be too long before I'm a bit wary of renewing the experiment with the pin. Nothing's moving yet, Ryan, but I can feel it. Looks like the doctors know what they're talking about after all.'

The depression that had hung around Siobhán since they returned from the cruise lifted and once again she became the forward looking positive woman she had been before the accident. If grit and determination had anything to do with it she'd conquer this. She had them in spades.

★ ★ ★

'Ryan. *Ryan!*'

He was in Siobhán's room before she'd completed the last syllable.

'It's okay, sis. It's okay.' He grabbed hold of her, trying to give her comfort, thinking she'd had a bad dream; no, not a dream, a nightmare.

'No, Ryan, no. It isn't that. Turn on the light. Quickly, turn on the light.'

It was three in the morning. He knew what the time was. Like most nights now he had lain awake staring at the ceiling, the only light in the room the reflection on the ceiling of the illuminated clock. Exhausted, he'd drop off for an hour or two and then spend the rest of the time in a futile attempt to get back to sleep.

What was wrong with Siobhán to make her cry out like that? He watched as she flung the duvet away.

'Look, Ryan, look.'

He focused on her feet and saw her toes move — only a little, but they definitely moved, on both feet. She burst into tears and there was certainly a constriction in his throat that hadn't been there before.

'I know they told us, I know they said it would be all right. But they didn't tell us when.'

'They didn't know, Ryan.'

He laughed joyfully. 'I didn't believe in them, Siobhán. I was never really sure they meant it.'

She wiped her face and stared at him in amazement. 'And after you kept telling me it'd be okay. I'll never believe another word you say.' She smiled up at him. 'I'd have woken you anyway, maybe just not so violently. I needed the loo. I can't walk yet, but maybe soon. Maybe soon.'

Ryan carried her there and back and went to make coffee. Both were too overwrought to sleep again that night. There was no further change in the small hours but it was a start. Yesterday's weather gave way to a glorious sunrise and a clear blue sky. The significance wasn't lost on either of them. They got transferred to voicemail three times because they couldn't wait to see the specialist and they tried far too early, before anyone was in the office. When they did finally get through they had to contain their agitation when he said he didn't need to see Siobhán immediately, though an appointment was made for later in the week. Ryan wanted to tell the world. Above all he wanted to tell Beth. He pushed the thought away.

* * *

'It's like I told you. Everyone's body heals at a different rate. Try not to be impatient,' they were told, though the consultant appreciated this was vain advice. 'It will happen in its own time. Don't try to run before you can walk, Siobhán; but I promise you, you will run.' This was the time he liked best. When a patient knew, really knew they were going to get better. This young woman had been through so much. It was lovely to see the smile back on her face.

Her progress after that was rapid and in Ryan's opinion nothing short of miraculous. Her legs had shut down, allowing them time to heal without further trauma, but the process was advanced now and the question was no longer would she walk again, but *when* she would walk again. Siobhán went through a period when she learned to use a frame, then crutches before she finally progressed to sticks. The muscles had become somewhat wasted and she needed to build them up again. No one was ever more diligent than she in doing their exercises.

She knew she would have to make a new life for herself and she realised there were still huge obstacles to overcome, not the least of which was the question mark hanging over Ryan while the Garda were conducting their investigations. She'd accepted that she'd never see Niall again; that Caitlan was lost to her forever; that the child she'd been carrying had lost its chance of life before it was even born. She realised she, too, might have died in the mangled wreck. Siobhán had a choice: give herself over to despair or begin to function again just like her legs were beginning to function. It was a no-brainer.

12

'I can't believe it's December already. Are you up for organising the celebrations again?'

'Just you try and take it away from me and see what you get, Simon. Do you want a theme this year or just a straightforward party?'

'Beth, when have I ever interfered with you when it comes to organising an event? It's what you do. Just let me know what you decide. The only thing I really need to know upfront is whether you're planning an office party, a restaurant, a pub or a dirty weekend.'

'Do I look like I need a dirty weekend?' She smiled, running her hand over her now somewhat expanded tummy.

'Might be just the thing for you. However, I have to agree it's not quite suitable for all of us. Linda and I would end up being divorced and as she's the love of my life I wouldn't like that very much. Unless she wanted me to be her partner, in which case we don't need everyone else from the office being there. Howard's just broken up with Jasper, you're without a partner at the moment, and some of the other office relationships are a bit dubious, so perhaps a dirty weekend isn't such a good idea after all.'

'Simon, I really believe your first suggestion was best; you know, the one where you said you'd leave it all to me.'

Beth loved her job and the people she worked with. They were more like family than work associates, maybe because she had no brothers or sisters of her own, and laughing with all of them, not just Simon, was the best therapy she could have. Organising the firm's Christmas party had always fallen naturally to her, and she probably would have resisted quite strongly if anyone had tried to take it away from her.

'A restaurant I think, Simon. Which of us doesn't like to go out for a meal?'

'Not you, that's for sure. Look at you. You look like you've eaten a football.'

'Very funny. Lunch, not dinner, what with Howard's situation and one or two of the others. Means we don't have to invite partners and as Linda is nominally a member of staff . . . '

'Yes, I'd like to see anyone trying to stop her coming.'

' . . . I think that's probably the best solution. I get free rein though, decorating the office?'

'Well we haven't had a bad year. I think we can probably run to some streamers and a few balloons. No breathing in the helium though. I remember the last time.'

'But I love the squeaky voices. You're such a killjoy.'

She, too, remembered the last party. She was struggling to remember it was almost a year ago.

'Oh my goodness! I had no idea,'

Beth had said as everyone shouted 'Surprise!' when she'd come back to the office after being sent on an errand she later realised was contrived. All the usually-for-Christmas decorations were out, plus a few extras. A large banner announcing 'THIRTY YEARS OLD' was stuck at a crooked angle on the wall.

'Happy birthday, Beth!' they'd yelled, and she'd joined in blowing up the rest of the balloons. They had a lot more fun with the helium used to inflate them, however; a spot-on impression of the Chipmunks being Howard's contribution to the squeaky voices, hence Simon's reference now to the helium. It was the best party she'd ever had, except that Gerry wasn't there.

'I did ask him, Beth. He couldn't make it back in time,' Simon had explained.

Gerry and Beth celebrated at their favourite restaurant two days later but it wasn't the same at all; not for her thirtieth. He slid a long box across the table towards her.

'Sorry it's late.'

'Gerry, it's beautiful. I love it.'

And it was, but even the very expensive bracelet couldn't and didn't make up for his absence.

Over the years they'd accumulated quite a collection of bits and baubles, but the tree was always a real one. Both she and Simon insisted on it and even the office cleaner, who also came to the party of course, didn't seem to object to clearing up the profusion of pine needles that seemed to be around for weeks after the tree had gone.

★ ★ ★

Christmas was looming large for the Donovans as well. Neither was looking forward to it, and it looked like being a rather low-key affair until their parents insisted they come and stay, and in all honesty they were both grateful for the summons. Pat and Pat Donovan — it happens in Ireland — lived in a country village where Church was the centre of the community, and they really knew how to celebrate and to honour the occasion. Neither brother nor sister had been home for Christmas for a very long time; Ryan because he didn't do religion, and Siobhán because there'd been an almighty row the first year of her marriage when Niall had well and truly upset the whole family. Sadly and too often there are still times when Catholic and Protestant just do not mix. In their own home Siobhán and Niall had decided there would be no overt observance. What each did privately contented them and was sufficient, but in the midst of a very Roman Catholic celebration Niall had been unable to keep his mouth shut. The experiment had never been repeated. At home they'd decorated the house, but each had gone to their own church. It suited them well enough. After Caitlan was born they took it in turns. Siobhán was always free to go to Midnight Mass while Niall looked after their daughter.

'It'll be good to see Gran again. How old is she now? Ninety-two?'

'And she's still living at home with Mam and Dad, and Mam looking more like her every day. I can see myself in years to come looking exactly the same.'

'Not you, Siobhán. You're the image of our dad.'

Siobhán's walking was improving all the time now, though her muscle tone wasn't yet what it should be, and she always carried a stick when she left the house. At home she just leaned on whatever furniture happened to be to hand, or the wall if that was nearer.

'I bet Gran doesn't use a stick, stubborn old lady. I love her to bits.'

'And wouldn't she love to hear you call her stubborn, Siobhán? Though she'd deny it in a whisker of course.'

Ryan tried hard not to wonder what Beth would be doing this Christmas, and Siobhán put memories of the last one and her daughter's excited squeals as far to the back of her mind as she could. She wasn't very successful. How could she be?

Ryan drove his sister to Ballybeg in time for dinner on Christmas Eve and they all went to Midnight Mass, even Gran.

'If I can't pay my respects to the Good Lord I might as well give up now.'

No one dared argue with her, but her grandchildren stood one at each elbow as she walked into the church, though Gran was convinced she was supporting Siobhán and not the other way around. Christmas Day was just like when they were children. Mam had made far too much food; what mother doesn't? And nobody mentioned the awful year they'd had. If Pat Donovan cast an anxious glance at her daughter from time to time, or her husband was overly cheerful, it passed unremarked upon. In the end they stayed the extra days, and nowhere at midnight on New Year's Eve was the toast more sincere than the one they raised their glasses to in the Donovan household.

*   *   *

Beth's Christmas lunch was a huge success. There were eleven of them, so they squashed around a large round table that should really only have seated ten, but nobody minded. At least with a round table you can see everyone, even if you have to shout at them to make yourself heard. It didn't take anyone long to get into party mood. Crackers were pulled, silly hats donned, and they'd got through three bottles of wine before the starters were even served. Beth of course wasn't drinking alcohol, but she was in that lovely world expectant mothers often visit where everything around her felt warm and lovely.

'What are you doing for Christmas, Howard?' one of the party asked.

Wrong question. All the light went out of his face and silent tears crept from the corners of his eyes. Beth rushed to fill the gap.

'I'm going to my parents' tomorrow. They like to make a big thing of it so I usually try to get there for Christmas Eve. Hey, why don't you come with me this year? I know they'll be delighted.'

The invitation crossed her lips before she'd even finished the thought, but she was glad. Like a clown, Howard's mouth turned from down to up and a smile transformed his face. She knew her parents wouldn't mind and they knew Howard of old, so there would be no suspicion that he was 'the man'. She needed to tread a little warily when asking her next question.

'Are you still at the flat? Shall I pick you up at eleven?'

'Yes, the flat is mine. I didn't see why I should be the one to move out.'

It was good to see him showing some spirit. Spirit would get him through a broken heart; not that Beth had found it helped her very much, but she was still hoping.

Christmas at home had never changed. Dad, a pipe man since his teens, couldn't see his habit in the same light as cigarette smoking, and to be fair there were a lot who agreed with him. The house had the lovely tobacco smell that reminded Beth of her childhood, mingling as it did with wood smoke from the fire. He wrung Howard's hand and the two of them sat down to watch sport on the television while Beth and her mother went into the kitchen for those last-minute preparations. There wasn't really anything left to do. Mother just wanted to make sure daughter was okay, and there was no denying pregnancy suited her.

'You must be counting the weeks now, Beth, if not the days.'

'Not the days, Mum. I've still got three months to go, but I have to admit I can't wait. This is the best thing that's ever happened to me.'

'I don't suppose . . . '

'No, Mum. Don't even go there.'

'Okay. I know when to give in. Are you staying for New Year? We'd love to have you; Howard too. It must be hard for him this year.'

'Yes, he and Jasper had been together for over four years, much longer than me and Gerry.'

'Don't talk to me about that man.'

'You're right, Mum. I don't want to talk about him either. Yes, I'm pretty sure I can speak for Howard. We'd love to stay.'

13

'It's time I thought about moving back to my flat, Siobhán. I've been putting it off for a while now, not for your sake but for mine.'

'You can stay here forever as far as I'm concerned.'

'I can't, sis. You know I can't. While I'm here you're too busy worrying about me, looking after me, to get on with your own life. It sounds hard, I know, and I'm so proud of how far you've come; but the truth is you still have one giant step to take. You have to go it alone.'

'I know it, Ryan.'

'There's another truth here, though, that maybe you don't know or won't acknowledge. It's been a long time since you leaned on me, Siobhán. It's nearly a year since the accident. You're ready to move on. I'm still in the same place I was when we left the ship. I haven't moved anywhere. She haunts my dreams. I can't get her out of my mind, day or night. Until the police finish their investigation I can't go anywhere, not for any length of time at any rate. I know that. Once it's all over, once my innocence is proved, I've decided . . . '

This was what the conversation was building up to. This was what Ryan had been going over in his head, over and over, and now the time had come to tell Siobhán.

' . . . I'm going abroad. I'm going to start again where nobody knows me; where I'm not haunted by Beth's face wherever I go.'

'But Beth was never here, Ryan. Nowhere in the world is going to be any different from here while you still carry her in your heart.'

An irrefutable truth, he knew, but he had to do something. Ryan had had girlfriends before. He'd even thought of moving in with one of two of them, but when it came to it he knew he wasn't committed enough. Love had never touched him until a diminutive curly-haired blonde with rosebud lips had smiled up at him and stolen his heart.

'Have you never thought you might try to find her, Ryan? See if she's happy?'

'She's with another man, Siobhán. I was just a shipboard romance, remember,' he answered bitterly. Those beautiful eyes looked bleakly at her. 'But it seemed so real, sis. Like nothing that had ever happened before; like nothing I'd ever known.'

'Stay a while longer, Ryan. Wait till the year is over, just until then, and I won't ask you for any more.'

'Okay, sis, just until then. There's a convention I ought to go to in London though. I didn't mention it before, but I think it's safe to leave you for a couple of days now if that's okay.'

'Of course it is.' Siobhán hesitated. 'Have you heard anything recently?'

He knew what she meant. The fact

that he was going away had brought the case to the front of her mind, but he was free to travel; no charges had yet been laid against him. He never discussed the inquiry with her. After all, she'd lost everything that day. The fact that her own brother was being investigated for the murder of her husband and child was outside anything either of them would ever have expected to have to deal with.

'The case is pending; the investigation ongoing. That's all they'll tell me. I wish I knew who the bastard was who has it in for me so badly he'd incriminate me in a murder charge. I've never asked you, Siobhán. Do you believe there's any truth in it?'

'Ryan, I remember the boy who cried when his pet mouse died; who couldn't put an injured squirrel out of its misery because he couldn't kill another living creature. No, Ryan, I never have, not for a single moment.'

★ ★ ★

Beth was working from home most of the time now. Simon had linked her laptop to the office network and she had direct access to anything going on there. Sometimes she'd go in to look at the drawings that were being drafted. It was easier to work on them at full size than on a small screen, but being in the cosiness of the annexe was much more comfortable for her now that her body was swelling to a size she was amazed her skin could accommodate, and Simon brought home any hard copy she needed. There was a printer at home if she needed anything in a hurry.

'I've asked Claire to do next week's presentation, Beth. She was fine when she substituted for you last year.'

Beth was quite happy for Claire to demonstrate the proposal. She felt she wouldn't be seen to carry enough authority in her present state. It had been tough enough before to convince a room full of people that a tiny blonde had planned down to the last detail the proposal being put before them, or the reception they were attending. A tiny blonde in the advanced stages of pregnancy certainly wouldn't do it.

'I would like to come with you though, Simon. This will be my last full on project before the baby arrives. This is a different sort of baby and I'm still responsible for its conception and I'd like to be there.'

'If you think you'll be okay, of course come.'

'I promise not to go into labour in the car. It's only a couple of hours to London. I've still got weeks and weeks to go. I'll be fine.'

★　★　★

'Beth, you're as white as a sheet. What's the matter?' asked Claire. 'Oh my God, you haven't started have you?'

'No. Claire, just get me out of here quickly, please.'

Claire took Beth to her room and thanked the powers that be they were staying overnight and the room was available. There was still an hour to go before the presentation, and if Beth was ill Simon would just have to carry it on his own. She gave all her attention to her friend.

'What is it? You look like you've see a ghost.'

'I have.'

'Are you hallucinating?'

'I wish. No, Claire, it's Ryan. He's in the convention hall.'

'What! Are you sure? No, sorry; silly question. Do you want to see him?'

'No, he mustn't know. It's just . . . it was such a shock. Thank goodness he had his back to me.'

Claire didn't like to ask how Beth could be so sure it was Ryan if she couldn't even see his face; but she knew, because Beth had told her, that he was well over six feet tall. If you know someone well you can always recognise them by their stature — and Beth knew Ryan very well indeed.

'I wonder what he's doing here. He certainly isn't on our list.'

'There are a couple of functions going on, Claire. Maybe he's wandered into the wrong one. What am I going to do? I so desperately want to see him, you know that, but I daren't. I can't believe he's actually here.' Her voice had risen in panic.

'I'll go back down and do a bit of sleuthing.' In spite of the seriousness of the situation, Claire was quite naturally curious to meet the man who'd turned her best friend's life upside down. 'I won't suggest you relax. I don't want you throwing that rather nice bedside lamp at me.'

Claire had no trouble picking Ryan out of the crowd. She went straight up to him. 'Hi, I'm Claire. S & L Presentations. Are you here for us today?'

'Ryan Donovan,' he said, shaking hands with her. 'No, I'm with the other lot. They've finished now and I'm just killing time before catching a plane. I have to fly back home, but it's much more pleasant waiting here than in the airport lounge. Do you work in London?'

Claire could see immediately why Beth had fallen so hard. There was a natural charm about the man that she would defy anyone not to respond to. She remembered Beth's first description. Adonis. She couldn't argue with that, except she'd always pictured Adonis with fair hair.

'No, but we often come here because it's more convenient for our clients.'

'Where are you from then?'

'Oxford,' Claire said, praying that Ryan wouldn't connect her name and city with Beth. She prayed in vain. There was a sudden, controlled but definitely there, intake of breath. She waited, wondering if he would ask her if she knew Beth. Of course she wasn't the only Claire in the world, but coincidence is a funny thing, and she did know Beth had mentioned her to Ryan when she'd explained to him why she was on board.

'It's not as big as London but it's a

beautiful city. Have you ever been there?' she asked, trying to fill the gap.

'No, but I used to know someone who lives there. I lost her.' He looked so bleak. His eyes had that same look Beth's had when she returned from the cruise.

'I'm sorry. Will you be staying for the dinner later?'

'No, it's like I said. I'm marking time before my flight. I have to get back to my sister.'

'Is she ill?'

'She has been. She was in an accident and couldn't walk for a while, but she's getting better every day now. I still don't like to leave her for long periods at a time though.'

'What a lovely brother you must be. It's been really nice meeting you, Ryan. If you'll excuse me now, I have to mingle.'

Claire stopped to speak to Simon in case Ryan was watching her. It wouldn't do if he saw her rush straight from the room when she'd just said she was circulating.

'I have to go up to see Beth, Simon. She's not feeling too well.'

'Not the baby!'

'No, she'll be fine. Just give me a few minutes. Are you okay to carry on without me for a bit?'

'No problem. Tell her I hope she feels better soon.'

Claire raced back upstairs reflecting that it was more than unlikely she would be.

'Did you see him? What did he say?'

Claire repeated the conversation as best she could. Beth gasped in the same place Ryan had, anticipating the question he didn't ask. When Claire got to the part where Ryan had said 'I lost her,' Beth burst into tears.

'You're safe enough, as long as you keep out of the way for a while. I'll let you know when he's gone.'

'How did he look, Claire?'

'I've never seen such sadness in a person's eyes, except yours.'

Claire went down to work. Ryan had left the hall and she didn't see him again. She had to assume he'd gone. Just as well. Though she'd never have betrayed her friend's trust, it would have been difficult not to probe further, and that could only have set him wondering.

★   ★   ★

On the advice of the midwife, Beth had taken to catnapping during the day; not that she could have stopped herself if she'd tried, she was so tired. She didn't usually go to bed, finding the sofa a perfectly good substitute. One early February afternoon she awoke suddenly to find it was pitch-black outside. The sky had been a clear blue when she'd snuggled down under the fleece blanket and there were no lights on in the room. Beth was surprised at how dark it was and a shiver ran through her. She folded her hands to protect her unborn baby and realised that tears were streaming out of her eyes and into her ears because she was flat on her back.

She had been dreaming again.

Where are you, Ryan? Have the Garda got any further? Are you in prison? Did I do the right thing?

Though it wasn't unusual for her to have these conversations with herself, it was the first time she'd woken up crying. Since seeing him a few weeks ago, her sleep was if anything even more restless. Was it the baby or was it the shock of him being there? Probably both.

Beth had spent many hours during her pregnancy trawling the internet for information about the case. She only had Ryan's name to go on — and of course, Siobhán's, though she hadn't known her surname as she'd travelled under her maiden name on the cruise — but that should have been sufficient to track anything down. She'd found references to the accident and horrific photos to go with them. It seemed impossible to her that Siobhán had survived such a crash. There was never any reference to an impending trial, or even any suggestion it would come to trial, though her dreams were full of it.

Beth thought often about the girl who had her brother's laughing eyes. Were they laughing still? How had she been able to laugh after what she'd been through? What would she give to see the two of them now? She was quite sure neither would want to have anything to do with her. She'd been unbelievably cruel to Ryan and, though it had seemed to be her only course of action at the time, there was no reason why he should ever want to see her again. Siobhán must hate her for what she'd done to her brother. What contempt she must feel when she remembered Beth promising to make Ryan's happiness her life's work. The only good thing that had come out of the chance encounter in London was the knowledge that Siobhán was on the mend, physically at least.

14

Ryan knew her waking torment never left her, but then Siobhán's nightmares started again.

'Don't go, Ryan. Please don't leave me; I don't think I can do this without you.'

Siobhán was calm now as she pleaded with him to stay. They were facing one another across the kitchen table, each cradling a mug of hot coffee. It was four o'clock in the morning and Siobhán's screams had summoned Ryan instantly. Not this time the excitement of manoeuvrability. This time pain was etched in tiny little lines around her eyes.

'How long has it been going on?'

'It's been getting worse for the last week or so. Maybe it's because it's almost a year now. The date jumps out at me every time I look at the calendar. I don't know.'

'You've been amazing, Siobhán; perhaps a bit too amazing. Externally you've done a great job of coping, but heaven knows what you've got locked inside. You're still taking the tablets?'

Ryan was referring to the medication she'd been given, not for her physical injuries but for the mental trauma.

'Yes, of course, but the sweats have come back. The bed is drenched. And, Ryan . . . ' She hesitated and he gave her time to pull herself together again. 'I feel as if my legs are pinioned again. Caitlan is screaming in the back and I can't get to her. And then she stops. That's the worst part. The silence. I'll never be able to come to terms with the fact that she died without my arms to comfort her; that she suffered pain no child should have to suffer; that no one should have to suffer.'

Niall hadn't uttered a sound. For him death had been instantaneous, and it was a long time, Ryan knew, before Siobhán could stop wishing it had taken her too.

'I can feel the heat between my legs too, as my unborn baby followed its father and sister into the next world.'

'You need help, sis. I told you months ago you couldn't do this on your own. I'm making an appointment with the doctor first thing tomorrow and I'm coming with you. This time when he recommends therapy I want you to listen. We have to rid you of these demons if we can, give your grief another way out.'

'But you'll stay? Just a bit longer, Ryan; just till I learn to cope again.'

It wasn't like Siobhán to use emotional blackmail. She was desperate, and there was no way he would leave her while she still needed him.

'What do you think? Of course I'll stay, unless you want to go to Mam and Dad for a while.'

'I couldn't, Ryan. I can never forget when I'm there that I married away from the faith; that to them Niall wasn't my husband, he was my Protestant husband.'

'How much heartache and bloodshed has there been on this earth in the name of religion? Stupid. Stupid!' Ryan vented his anger.

'And every one of them preaching peace!'

'Have you thought about work?'

'Work?'

'A job, Siobhán. While you were paralysed it was out of the question, but now . . . Maybe you've been spending too much time on your own. I don't know what you do with yourself every day when I'm at work, but I'd go spare if I only had the television and books to rely on.'

Siobhán cringed at the word 'paralysed'. It still had the power to hurt, but Ryan could be right. She hadn't worked since she'd been pregnant with Caitlan, but there was no reason why she couldn't and every reason why she should.

'You're right. And you're right about the television; but I have read quite a few good books.'

Beth sat sipping tea, knowing Simon well enough to realise he was feeling uncomfortable, which he confirmed when he said: 'I know this is absolutely the worst time in the world to pick, and I don't know how to ask you, but . . . '

'What is it, Simon? Come on, out with it.'

'Well, you know Mum's not been great the past few weeks.'

'Yes, of course I do. Is anything wrong? Has she got worse?'

'They don't think she can manage at home any longer, Beth. I know we said it was open-ended, but I'm afraid we need to move her and Dad into the annexe. It's a lot sooner than we'd anticipated, but . . . '

'Of course. Don't be silly. It's yours after all. How soon do you need me to go?'

Simon looked a bit embarrassed but the truth was he didn't really have any choice. 'As soon as you can make other arrangements, Beth. If they're here Linda can keep an eye on them, do the shopping and the cooking, all the things Mum can't do for herself anymore. Dad, being an old-fashioned sort of man, is about as much use — though I hate to admit it — as absolutely nothing at all.'

Beth tried not to let him see how wrecked she was. After all, he and Linda had been incredibly good to her.

'Don't worry; if I can't find something quickly I can always move in with my parents for a while. I know it's further away, but as long as I have my laptop it shouldn't be too much of a problem. Anyway, I'll get on to it right away. It's, what, Wednesday today? Will it be okay if I hang on till the weekend?'

'Yes, of course it will. Is there anything I can do to help?'

'Not unless you know anyone who wants to flat-share.'

'I may just be able to help you there.'

Serendipity or not, that was how Beth found herself moving into the spare room in Howard's flat. It was an arrangement that suited both of them. Jasper had been the homemaker half of their partnership and Howard, efficient as he was at work, was as helpless as a lot of other men when it came to housekeeping — Simon's father for example. Beth was happy to keep house for them both and though she'd rather not have had to share a bathroom, it was a better solution for the time being that finding a place of her own in a hurry. That was how mistakes were made. When the time came for her to choose a home for her and the baby she wanted it to be perfect.

Neither she nor Howard were likely to make any undue demands on the other, and both being sociable by nature found after Beth moved in that it was rather nice to have company in the evenings. Getting a take-away was also nicer if you had someone to share it with.

'I don't know what they put in the curry but it's given me terrible stomach cramps. You okay, Howard?'

'Fine. Too spicy for you, maybe? Do you want me to get you a glass of water?'

'Please. It might just help push it down. Oh God, that hurts. That's better. Thanks, Howard, I'm sure the water's helping.'

'Just as long as you're okay.'

'Yes I'm f . . . Ow. I'm never getting anything from that take-away again.'

'I've never had a problem before. Are you sure you're okay, Beth? You look a bit odd.'

'I don't feel too good to be honest. Oh my God. Howard! You don't think . . . ?'

'I'm phoning the hospital right now.'

'But I've still got five weeks to go. I can't be having the baby now.'

'Maybe you should try telling the baby. Meanwhile I'm phoning the hospital.'

Beth tried not to be frightened as Howard drove her to the hospital. Howard also tried not to be frightened;

Beth could see that. It was a situation in which presumably he'd never expected to find himself.

'I'm so sorry to put you through this, Howard.'

'Look, Beth. I don't know what happened after you and Gerry split up but it's obvious this isn't his baby, not unless the gestation period's gone up by a few months. You're a nice girl, and if I ever get my hands on the man who's left you to go through this alone I'll . . . well, I'm not violent by nature but I know what I'd like to do. Anyway, I just wanted to say don't worry. I'll look after you. They'll look after you at the hospital. We're nearly there. How are the contractions? Are they coming often?'

Howard's questions came in short bursts, a sure sign of his own anxiety, but they made it to the hospital and Beth was wheeled away. It was assumed by everyone there that Howard was Beth's partner and he chose not to correct them.

'It's going to be a while, Mr . . . ?'

'Carter.'

'It's going to be a while but Beth has definitely gone into labour. You're welcome to stay but it's likely to be a long time. We could call you at home if you want.'

'No, I want to be here. Is there anywhere I can get a cup of coffee? It was all rather sudden.'

The nurse told Howard where the machine was and he raced off and raced back again, clutching the polystyrene cup and hoping he hadn't missed anything. Missed anything? The nurse smiled kindly as he asked the question.

'It really is going to be some time, Mr Carter. There are plenty of magazines. If I were you I'd settle down for the long wait.'

'Thank you.'

'You can go and sit with her, you know. She isn't ill; she's just having a baby. I expect she'd appreciate you holding her hand. Come with me, I'll show you the way.'

Beth was sitting up in bed looking worried.

'The contractions aren't coming very often but it's definitely started. I think they might be a bit concerned about the size of the baby. I'm not very big . . . no me, you big idiot, not my stomach,' she said as he glanced down at her sizable bulge. 'As it's obviously not going to full term, they would expect it to be smaller than they'd like. They've told me not to worry, but . . . ' Beth looked at Howard out of frightened saucer-like eyes. 'Please stay with me. I don't want to do this alone.'

'I have absolutely no intention of going anywhere. If you don't want me in the room with you I'll wait outside. Apart from that, you're stuck with me. Now just try to relax. You're in good hands.'

And so began the longest night of Howard's life.

★ ★ ★

'Would you mind waiting outside, Mr Carter? I won't be long.'

'They keep asking me, Beth, but I think it's more a command than a request,' he said on one occasion when he'd returned to her side. 'What on earth are they doing every time I go out, if it's not too personal a question?'

'It's just observation. You know, checking blood pressure, temperature, whatever. Are you okay?'

'Of course I am. It's you we have to worry about. Get some rest while you can.'

Beth tried to relax and to a certain extent she succeeded. She apologised profusely though, several times, when yet another contraction caused her to clutch Howard's hand quite fiercely, jerking him awake from his own fitful dozing. They weren't coming at even intervals but they were increasing in intensity.

'Why don't you both go for a little walk in the corridor? That sometimes helps get things going.'

At first it was a welcome change from doing nothing, but it soon became quite tedious. So they sat, the two of them, on a couch in the alcove at the far end. Beth knew Howard was trying to take her mind off her discomfort when he started talking to her about Jasper, but all he succeeded in doing was upsetting himself.

'I thought we were so happy together. He'd even given up work because he liked being at home, cooking and cleaning; doing, you know, all the things that housewives do.' He smiled ironically at the phrase but Beth could see that he was bewildered. 'I'm earning good money. He never had to worry about anything. What did I do wrong?'

'You're a lovely man, Howard; a very special man. I'm sure you didn't do anything wrong; it's just that sometimes people's feelings change.'

'I wonder where he is now. He went back to his mum and dad — I told you, didn't I — but he wouldn't like sharing a kitchen, that's for sure. I spoke to Rita a while ago, you know, to wish her Merry Christmas. We'd been good friends and she was like a mother to me too. She said he wasn't there anymore and he'd asked her not to give me a forwarding address. After all we've been to each other! I only wanted to make sure he was okay.'

Beth watched as the tears rolled down Howard's cheeks, and his hands gripped hers just as tightly as she ground his fingers together when another contraction hit her unexpectedly.

'I think I'd better go back to bed for a while. I'm absolutely exhausted and I've still got a long way to go. Are you sure you don't mind staying?'

'We've done this one already, Beth. I'll be here when you wake up.'

As they walked back along the corridor Beth's waters broke. Howard left her for a moment to go in search of a nurse and a wheelchair. Beth blanched when she saw the chair. She could tell Howard and the nurse were wondering if she was having another contraction, but it was the sight of the wheelchair that had distressed her. She knew Siobhán was making progress, but Beth could only picture her as she was on the ship. Where was Siobhán now? Where was Ryan? *Not here, because I haven't told him — haven't allowed him to be here when his child comes into the world.*

Oh Ryan, she groaned inwardly, and then outwardly as the contractions came again.

15

Siobhán and Ryan were sitting at the kitchen table discussing Siobhán's job prospects. It was nearly five o'clock and there didn't seem to be much point in going back to bed.

'It's probably not a good idea for you to come and work in the factory. It's where Niall worked, where you met him. Too many painful memories, as if you didn't have enough to deal with already. Anyway, thank goodness the place runs like clockwork. Sometimes I wonder if they even need me.'

'Every business needs a figurehead, Ryan, even if they're not doing any work.'

They smiled at each other for the first time since Siobhán had woken screaming.

'Have a little respect for your big brother. Of course I'm doing work. It's just that the place is like a well-oiled machine and unlike Dad before me I don't have any difficulty delegating.'

'Well you won't be delegating anything to me. I'm sure I'll be able to find work somewhere other than the family business. I wouldn't want you to be accused of nepotism.'

Ryan was more pleased than he let her see at how she was ready and willing to take on a job. Because of her injuries neither of them had even thought about it before, but she'd been fairly mobile for some time now; she'd even discarded the stick. She'd just been drifting along, really. Aimlessly. What aim would she have after all that had happened to her? Somehow though she knew she had to build a life for herself. She'd do it, too. They came from tough stock, the Donovans. *Look at me*, Ryan thought. *I've proved strong enough to put Beth out of my mind for at least two minutes at a time each day.*

Though the day was just dawning

there was a buzz of activity outside the house.

'Listen to that,' said Siobhán. 'They've started celebrating already. It'll be mayhem before lunchtime.'

'Sure the parade starts earlier every year. Mind you, it's grand to have something to celebrate. I'm meeting the lads later for some of the magic black brew. Why don't you come with me?'

'I will, Ryan. I might even have a half myself.'

'You'll need it, and more besides, if Paddy comes out with the old joke again — and I don't see why this year should be any different from all the ones that have come before.'

'And what old joke would that be, Ryan?'

'Are you sure you want to hear this? Okay, here goes. When the Irish say that St Patrick chased the snakes out of Ireland, what they don't tell you is that he was the only one who saw any snakes!'

'That's a joke? I've changed my

mind. I don't think I'll come after all, if that's the standard of the entertainment.'

'Oh no, Siobhán, it gets much worse than that.'

Ryan was relieved that Siobhán seemed to have put off her depression for the time being. He realised there was no way he'd be able to get hold of the doctor this particular day for anything other than an emergency; and in any case, if Siobhán was positive about looking for a job, it might prove to be all the therapy she'd need. Nevertheless, he was glad there was something to act as a diversion, and a pretty big diversion at that.

Later in the day Siobhán and Ryan were at the pub enjoying a Guinness at exactly the same time as Beth was giving birth to her son. Ryan didn't know it but he was wetting his baby's head. Beth, exhausted and relieved it was all over, smiled at the irony when one of the nurses whispered, 'Happy St Patrick's Day, Beth.' There could be only one name for her son.

★　★　★

In the hours after the birth Beth was distraught. Her baby had been taken away and she didn't know why. She'd only held him for a few moments. They'd told her he was fine but she knew it wasn't normal procedure to separate a newborn from his mother.

'Oh, I'm glad you're here, Mr Carter. It's best I talk to both of you.' A doctor; one they hadn't seen before. 'The baby is smaller than we'd like, though in itself that wouldn't be too much of a concern. However he's having difficulty breathing. That's why we've had to take him away from you for the time being. We thought it best to put him in an incubator; help him along a bit. There's a concern his lungs aren't fully formed, so we want to give him all the help we can. You can see him, of course, but I'm afraid you won't be able to hold him for a while.'

Howard had thought Beth couldn't grip his hand any tighter than when she was in labour. He was wrong. She screwed up her eyes, trying to squeeze back the tears.

'What about feeding him? He'll have to be fed.'

'Of course he will. We'll need you to express your milk; that will be the best thing for him now. Nurse will help you; show you how. Then you might like to sit with him for a while; maybe have a little sleep yourself. I'm afraid there's very little you can do for him at the moment, but try not to worry. He's in good hands.'

Beth looked helplessly at Howard. 'What shall we do, Howard? I don't know what to do.'

'Why don't we do what the doctor suggests? Let's go and sit with him for a while, then I'll go home and pick up a few things for you. Your bag wasn't packed and we came out in such a hurry you don't even have a toothbrush. Then I can come back later to see how he's getting on. In the meantime, would you like me to wait outside while you talk to the nurse about expressing your milk?'

She nodded at him, in a daze and not knowing which way to turn, so grateful that he was there to take charge, frightened to ask questions; afraid of what the answers might be, and asking herself whatever had possessed Jasper to give him up.

Patrick looked so tiny when they went to see him in the critical care unit. He was so close, but he seemed helpless in his life-support machine. He looked peaceful; almost as if . . . She couldn't even bear the thought. No holding back the tears now. Beth sobbed as though her heart was breaking, which indeed it was. Howard was no comfort to her. His own tears fell as fast as hers and they clung to each other in their despair.

'You can put your hand into the incubator, you know. Here, let me show you.'

Half of Beth's finger was the size of Patrick's hand, but as she moved underneath he grasped her finger as if he'd never let it go. She'd never known such magic. That one small touch was enough to raise her spirits, though she didn't give herself the luxury of hope.

'Why don't you go and get some rest? There's nothing you can do for the moment. We would like you to come back later, get some more milk from you. And I know you'll want to see Patrick again; touch him again. But for the moment you need to gather your strength.' The nurse was gentle but firm. The situation was taken out of Beth's hands. She felt as if she was in the way.

'If you think it best. I'll come back soon though.'

'Any time you like.'

'Howard, can you take me back to the ward before you go home?'

'Of course I will. You just do what you can to build yourself up. Patrick's going to need you to be strong. I won't be long. I'll probably be back before you even wake up.'

Beth doubted she'd be able to sleep, she was so worried, but exhaustion overwhelmed her and she fell into a deep slumber before Howard was even out of the door. He went back to the flat, packed the few things he thought Beth would need, and cleared away the remains of the curry. He was back at the hospital within two hours, before Beth had woken up.

'How is he, Nurse? He looked so tiny and helpless.'

Beth asked the same question practically as soon as she opened her eyes. They'd made their way straight to the care unit.

'How is he; how is my baby?'

'We've managed to give him a feed but I'm afraid he's struggling a bit. Why don't you come back to the ward with me and express some more milk? Then I'd like you to have a word with Staff Nurse.'

Terrified at her perceived inference,

210

Beth took one more look at Patrick before going with the nurse.

'You can see for yourself he's not too well. We're doing everything we can and he's fighting hard.' The pause that followed filled her with dread. 'But I think you must prepare yourself for the fact that he might not make it. We're moving him to the infirmary. They have better facilities there; more experience with this kind of problem. I can organise a bed for you. You might want to stay at the hospital — '

'While I'm waiting for him to die,' Beth blurted out before she could stop herself.

'We have every hope he will pull through this, Beth. Try not to despair. We've seen miracles many times before. He'll need your strength too. I don't know if you're a religious person, but now might be a good time to pray.'

Ryan, though almost a constant presence anyway, came unbidden into Beth's thoughts. He had a son he didn't know about, and now that son was fighting for his life. The reasons for keeping them apart were fast becoming irrelevant. She had to let him know. How could she do otherwise? His mobile number was still stored in her phone. She remembered when she'd used it on the ship. 'On my way,' she'd texted after the musical extravaganza evening, when he was waiting for her with a plate of food. Before she could change her mind she turned to Howard.

'Howard, will you please excuse me for a moment? I need to make a call.'

Beth went and sat on the couch in the alcove where she and Howard had waited for the baby the night before; it seemed so long ago now.

'Ryan. Ryan, it's Beth.'

'What? Who? I can't hear you. Don't you know it's St Patrick's Day? Who did you say it was?'

'It's Beth,' she shouted into the phone.

Ryan felt his knees buckle.

'Wait, wait, hold on — I'll take this

outside.' He rushed out of the pub, terrified she might hang up on him. Then he spoke, slowly and deliberately. 'What the devil do you mean, phoning me like this after all this time? Haven't you done enough damage?'

'Ryan, don't. You have every right, I know, but there's something I need to tell you.'

'Well you'd better get on with it then, so you can get out of my life again.'

Ryan's shock took the form of sardonic aggression, and who could blame him? He'd never been so vulnerable with another human being, and attack seemed to be his only method of defence.

'It's not quite that simple. You have a son, Ryan. He was born this morning. They're not sure if he's going to survive.'

This time Ryan actually stumbled. He'd never expected to hear from Beth again; had resigned himself to the fact that the love of his life was in his past life. He'd been hurt so badly he was never going to lay himself open to the possibility again.

'What are you saying? How do you know . . . ?'

'There's no doubt, Ryan. You are Patrick's father. I thought you might like to see him while you still can. They're transferring him to the Radcliffe Infirmary. It's not far from here. They think he might stand a better chance there. Will you come?'

'Just tell me where it is. I'll be there as quickly as I can.'

'Oxford. It's world-famous. You'll have no trouble finding it.'

'I'll text you when I have an ETA. In the meantime, hang on in there, Beth. I'll get to you as soon as I can.'

Those last kind words came from the Ryan she remembered. Once again she burst into tears.

★　★　★

As soon as she saw Ryan coming back Siobhán knew something was wrong.

'Got to go, guys,' she said to the group they'd both been standing with, and she moved to meet her brother as he came towards her. 'What is it, Ryan? Whatever's the matter?'

'It's Beth.' He stopped, not quite sure how to continue or even where to start.

'What? For goodness sake, Ryan, what?

'She's had a baby.'

'Yours!'

'She says.'

'Do you doubt her?'

'No. She wouldn't lie about something like that. Anyway, there are DNA tests. What would be the point? Why didn't she tell me?'

'And why is she telling you now?'

'They're not sure if he's going to make it, sis. She wants me to come; to see him before . . . in case . . . '

'Okay, let's get home. We can both start making phone calls. Not everything closes on St Patrick's Day. We'll get the first flight and be there in no time.'

215

'You're coming with me?'

'What do you think?'

In less time than they would have believed possible they were on their way. Ryan sent Beth a text telling her when he was due to land and to expect him at the hospital in however long it would take to check out and get there by cab from the airport. He didn't know but she would. He didn't trust himself yet to speak to her on the phone.

Siobhán and Ryan sat in silence for most of the journey. What was there to say? Nothing had prepared either of them for this eventuality. 'She's called him Patrick,' was one of the few comments he made.

'What's wrong with the baby?'

'She didn't say.'

They reached the hospital at ten o'clock that night. His son, Ryan learned, was barely fifteen hours old. Patrick had exchanged one critical care unit for another, and Beth was sitting by his incubator with his tiny hand once more clutching her finger. Ryan's heart melted as he watched them, and then a nurse came and beckoned him inside. Obviously he was expected.

He moved to stand beside Beth and got his first proper look at his son. Something very new welled up inside him, something he didn't know how to handle. Beth sat rigid beside him. *She can't even bear to be near me.* If only he'd known what was really going through her mind; how desperate she was to feel his arms around her, comforting her. Instead they behaved like two strangers.

'Would you like to . . . ?' Beth withdrew her hand and gave him her seat. He pushed his hand into the incubator with the gentleness she had learned to expect from him. Large finger stroked soft skin with absolute wonderment, and Beth couldn't help remembering what his touch felt like on her own body.

'Why didn't you tell me, Beth? How could you not tell me?'

'It's complicated.'

'Damn right it's complicated.'

'Shall we go outside while we talk?'

How well he remembered the softness in her voice, accentuated now in the presence of her child. They went outside where Howard and Siobhán were standing waiting. Beth looked up at Siobhán, tall by any standard, to find herself being regarded quizzically but, it seemed to her, kindly. Even in her own despair she longed to talk to her, this woman whom she'd felt could be her friend. Ryan's pent-up emotions got the better of him, and he marched up to Howard and downed him with one punch.

'This is the bastard you left me for? Was he there when my son was born?'

* * *

Beth stiffened. Ryan thought it was Gerry. Of course he did. Why should he think otherwise? She sympathised with his frustration but hated the violence.

218

'No Ryan, this is Howard — a good friend. And I think you owe him an apology.'

She moved out of the way, and Siobhán moved forward to look at the miracle that was a newborn child. Even wrinkled and premature, there was no doubting whose baby he was. An astonishingly large mop of dark hair crowned his tiny face.

'Is he breathing?'

'Yes, but only with help.'

On his feet again, Howard was rubbing his chin, and stepped back quickly as Ryan looked at him. He didn't want a repeat performance. Ryan reluctantly extended his hand.

'I'm sorry. I shouldn't have done that. You're with Beth now. It's none of my business.'

And before she could stop him Howard, thinking she was in need of protection from this, he had to admit, rather handsome man, said, 'Yes, I am and no, it isn't.'

16

'Can I talk to you, Ryan?'

They'd been looking at the baby through the observation window for some time when Siobhán touched her brother's arm. Beth was on the other side of the screen, her finger clasped in Patrick's tiny fist. Together Ryan and Siobhán moved away and Beth glanced up briefly as she watched them go. She bit her lip and turned back. She couldn't believe Siobhán had made such an amazing recovery and thought again how much she'd like to talk to her. Whether or not Siobhán would ever want to talk to her again was another matter, but her expression when she'd looked at Beth hadn't been hard. Maybe there was hope.

Siobhán came straight to the point. 'Ryan, we're obviously going to be here for a while and we don't have anywhere to stay. It's already nearly midnight. Why don't I go and find a corner somewhere; sort out some accommodation and maybe arrange to hire a car?'

'Good idea. Not the car, though. I'm quite happy to use a taxi while I'm here, and it'll be less hassle than trying to learn my way around.'

'You realise, don't you, we've been up since three o'clock this morning? You're going to need to get some sleep soon.'

'No!' He hadn't meant to speak sharply, least of all to his sister. 'No, I'll find a chair and catnap here. I'm not leaving him. Look, why don't you find somewhere and give me the details? You can go and get some rest and come back fresh tomorrow.'

'If that's what you want. I'm just going to take another look at my nephew before I go.'

They made their way back to find some kind soul had provided chairs for them outside the unit. Ryan was going to be able to take his nap right there, without leaving his son. Beth came out of the unit at Siobhán's gestured request, and Siobhán told them where she was going and that she'd be back in the morning. She also gave Beth her mobile number, and she tried not to read anything into it other than that Siobhán was at least prepared to speak to her. Ryan didn't speak to her at all; just sat there gazing at the little scrap of humanity whose existence he'd only been aware of for a few hours.

'Mr Carter, the baby isn't in any immediate danger. Why don't you take Beth for a coffee or something? Give yourselves a break. We'll call you if there's any change.'

Ryan felt bitterness in his gut. A nurse he hadn't seen before was talking to Howard as if he were the baby's father. Having been excluded for so long, he wasn't going to be excluded now. He was just about to put the nurse right when he realised that this wasn't the appropriate time, and the three of them made their way to the all-night coffee shop on the next floor down. Howard took Beth's arm in what Ryan thought was a very proprietorial manner, but in fact the poor girl was exhausted. It wasn't yet twenty-four hours since she'd given birth, and she was going through hell. Beth leaned on him heavily, not caring for the moment what Ryan thought.

The coffee revived all of them to some degree.

'We need to talk, Beth.'

'I'm not leaving.'

'It's okay, Howard. Perhaps it would be best if Ryan and I had a few minutes. I owe him that much at least.'

At the very least, Ryan thought.

'Just how long were you going to keep your little secret, Beth? Don't you think I had a right to know?'

'You had a right to know? Didn't I have a right to know you were involved in a murder inquiry? Just how long were you going to keep your little secret? How do you think I felt hearing about that; hearing it from someone else?'

The words were out before she could stop them and, much as she wished they'd never been spoken, they were out in the open now. She'd never have said anything if she hadn't been so tired, so stressed, so worried about the baby. She watched as his face contorted with something she took to be rage; but what she didn't know was that it was directed at himself and his profound regret that he hadn't confided in her when he had the chance. He fought to control his features and his temper. If there had ever been any way at all, even the tiniest glimmer of hope that they would resolve their problems, Beth felt she'd effectively killed it off with her impulsive response. *There's more than one kind of murder*, she reflected bitterly.

It's often been said that attack is the best method of defence and Ryan used it now. 'Is that what this was all about? The inquiry? I thought the accused was at least entitled to a fair trial. Obviously you tried, condemned and hanged me without a second thought.'

Beth stayed silent. After all, in spite of his protestations she still had no proof that he wasn't guilty. All her reasons for remaining quiet, for leaving him in the first place, still stood. Maybe it was for the best. There was no future for them, whatever happened to Patrick. Patrick!

'We need to get back to the baby. We've already been gone longer than I meant to.'

'Okay, Beth. Perhaps I can make an appointment with you to discuss his future. I'm not prepared to believe he isn't going to pull through this, and I want you to know I'm ready to do anything necessary to have my share of custody.'

Beth pulled up short from her headlong dash out of the café. 'You can't! You live in another country.'

'Oh, can't I? We'll just have to see about that. In the meantime I'm going to see my son. Sorry if I'm walking too fast for you — you'll just have to keep up as best you can.' With those words he swept out of the door, where Beth found Howard waiting for her, his mouth open in shocked surprise.

'I take it that didn't go too well then?'

'Howard, he wants partial custody. He wants to take my baby away.'

Though his loyalties would always be to Beth, Howard could quite understand why Ryan would want at the very least some access to his own child. He would himself, except he'd never be a father other than by proxy. He was already emotionally involved with the little chap who was fighting for his life on the floor above. He could barely imagine how it would feel if he were his own flesh and blood. Howard said none of this to Beth. He thought she had enough to deal with at the moment and needed all the support she could get.

'Maybe we should cross that bridge when we come to it. I'm here for you, Beth. You know that. But in the meantime let's go and do what we can to help the little fellow fight his giant battle.'

★   ★   ★

Siobhán arrived in the morning to find all three of them sitting where she'd left them. There was no change. Patrick was no worse but he was no better either. They were approached by one of the nurses.

'Your son is holding his own at the moment, Mr Carter.'

'Thank you, Nurse.' Ryan could contain himself no longer. 'But Patrick is not Mr Carter's son, he's mine.

The nurse had experienced many unusual relationships and moved with ease into apologising for the misunderstanding. 'It's important Beth gets some rest. She's been on the go ever since Patrick was moved from the hospital to the Infirmary; before, in fact. I'll arrange accommodation for her. She's in no fit state to go home yet, and in any case Patrick will benefit from his mother being here.'

Beth was beginning to resent every-thing being directed first through Howard and now Ryan.

'If you can find me a room I'd be very grateful. I'm not leaving my baby.'

'Of course. I'll get straight back to you as soon as it's organised.'

Ryan and Siobhán moved aside and put their heads together. Beth strained her ears but couldn't hear what they were saying. She wouldn't normally be so nosy, but whatever they were talking about undoubtedly affected her and her son.

'I think I'd like you to go back to Dublin if you don't mind, Siobhán. We're in for the long haul here, and although I said that the business was like a well-oiled machine, it does still need someone at the helm. You may not have worked there for years, but everyone knows you're on the board and you carry authority. Sod nepo-tism. I need you to filter any problems and keep me posted. Would you do that for me, sis?'

'I'd really prefer to stay with you, but it makes sense. What went wrong, Ryan? You can see there's nothing between Beth and Howard. It's obvious they're just good friends.'

'It wasn't obvious to the nurse. How can you be so sure?'

Siobhán smiled to herself but didn't enlighten him. She moved back to the other two and took Beth's arm, and the two of them moved away together.

'Beth, I don't know what went wrong and I know it's none of my business. Ryan's clammed right up. He won't talk to me about it, and you've obviously got more than enough to cope with at the moment. I just can't help remembering what you said to me that day on the ship, about making Ryan's happiness your life's work. No, don't cry. The way things are at the moment it looks as if you're never going to be able to work it out — and that would be a tragedy. If any two people were ever meant to be together it's you and Ryan.

That's all I have to say, Beth. I'm going back to Dublin, but if you ever need me you only have to call. You have my number.'

Beth felt like a drowning man who has been thrown a lifebelt.

17

'Why don't you go home and get some sleep, Howard. You've been here as long as I have and you'll have to go into work tomorrow.'

He looked across at Ryan and back to Beth, an unspoken question in his eyes.

'Don't worry. We won't come to blows, I promise you. You've been wonderful and I couldn't have managed without you. I don't have the words to thank you but I'll never forget what you've done for me during the past couple of days, and before come to think of it. But it's probably a good idea for me and Ryan to have a bit of space. This is both common ground and neutral territory.'

'If that's what you want. Don't hesitate though to call me if you need me. Give the little chap a stroke for me, will you?'

'I'm praying he's going to pull through, Howard. Then you'll be top of the list to have as many cuddles as you like.'

He left without another word, not saying goodbye to Ryan who was sitting with his son's fist clasped tightly round his finger. Beth went and sat next to him. Both of them had nodded off when they were disturbed by the nurse who suggested they might like to take the opportunity of a proper sleep.

'If he maintains this level we hope you'll be able to feed him yourself later. Let me show you where you can get some rest. Putting baby on the breast the first time isn't always as easy and straightforward as you might think. It will be strange for you and because he's being fed through a tube it will be strange for Patrick. He hasn't learned to suckle yet.'

They followed her meekly to a side room that had two beds in it. She held the door open. 'Get some sleep; both of you. I'll see you later.'

Beth and Ryan stepped into the room and she closed the door. The last time they'd been alone together, truly alone, was the night of Patrick's conception. Ryan turned his back on her and pulled off his shirt, glanced quickly over his shoulder, shrugged and stripped down to his underpants. He got into bed but not before Beth had an opportunity to see again the body that had haunted her dreams for so many months, the muscles that rippled with every move he made. Ryan was lying on his back with his hands clasped behind his head. He was smiling but it wasn't a nice smile. She removed only the clothes she had to before climbing into bed, acutely aware that she had not long given birth. She didn't know as she slipped under the duvet that Ryan had seen how heavy her breasts were, how beautiful to him, and how much he too couldn't dismiss the memory of their time together. He was damned if he'd let her know how attracted he was to her. How, even though there was no way he could forgive what she'd done, the pull was still there causing a fire in his blood and an ache in his heart.

Beth fell into immediate and blessed oblivion. Ryan lay staring at the ceiling; sleep eluding him even though he'd been awake for many hours now. Though his body hadn't been through the trauma hers had, nonetheless Siobhán waking in terror, the shock he'd received when Beth had called him and the arrangements and journey to Oxford, and all that had followed had taken their toll. Still he couldn't sleep. He was far too conscious that the object of his desire — yes, dammit, he still wanted her — was semi-naked and three feet away from him. *What kind of a fool are you, Ryan Donovan? She swept you aside and broke your heart. She kept her pregnancy from you; would have kept your son from you if she hadn't had a rush of guilt; if she could leave you once she could do it again.*

Yet the heat was in him, tugging at his loins and pulling at his heartstrings. *She'll not leave me again. I won't give her the opportunity. I wouldn't allow her that much satisfaction. But she's stuck with me anyway. If Patrick survives we will be inextricably tied. Never again though will I let her know how much she means to me.*

Ryan forced himself to think back on how hurt he'd been; found armour in these negative reflections. He decided that whatever arrangements were to be made regarding their son it would be on a business footing. He could do business. It was something he was good at. Relationships? Maybe not his strongest point. On that wry thought he finally fell asleep. Both were woken by the light that flooded into the room when the nurse opened the door.

'I'm sorry to disturb you but we wanted to try that first feed if you're up to it. I'll give you a few minutes to come to then I'll take you to the special baby care unit. I'll stay with you of course, help you along.'

Ryan and Beth looked at each other and both jumped out of bed, almost colliding in the middle then springing apart.

'I thought I'd only dozed off for a few minutes, but it's been hours,' she said, glancing at the clock on the wall.

'My tongue feels like it's covered in fur.'

'Mine too.'

Blood rushed into both their faces; neither wanted to think about tongues. They pulled their clothes on hurriedly and sat on the beds facing each other, waiting for the nurse to return. It was over five minutes later and each wondered why it is that hospitals think it takes so long to get dressed. They were taken back to the special unit where Patrick looked even smaller.

'Wash your hands and sit down, Beth, with your back supported. Comfortable? We'll begin by putting him in your arms so you can get used to holding him; see what it feels like; adjust to his weight. Then we'll see about feeding.'

She took their precious bundle and placed him in his mother's arms. Beth didn't know whether to laugh or cry. She looked over at Ryan, seeing only the top of his head as he gazed down at their baby. She looked down at Patrick. Ryan's was thicker, of course, but they both had the same mop of dark unruly hair.

'I'm almost frightened to hold him.'

'You're not the first new mother to say that and you won't be the last. Don't worry, you're doing fine. Shall we give his father a turn?'

Ryan looked terrified but sat down obediently. The nurse smiled. 'He's going to look pretty lost there, isn't he, but don't worry; they're a lot stronger than you think. It's Patrick's lungs we have to worry about not you holding him. Just be definite; make him feel secure.'

Ryan thought he'd lost his heart to Patrick from the moment he saw him but this was something different again. This living breathing child was part of him. He was finding it all very difficult to take in. He forgot himself for the moment and smiled warmly at Beth and the sun shone radiantly from her face. *I must remember not to let myself be drawn in.* He frowned and looked down again at his son. Beth felt as if she'd been slapped. The nurse seemed not to notice.

'Okay, while his dad is holding him let's adjust your clothing and we'll see if he'll feed. I know this is a very big moment for you but just try to relax.'

The nurse slipped the strap off Beth's left shoulder. Things had happened so quickly she didn't have a nursing bra yet. Her distended breast fell free and heavy and Patrick was taken from his father's hold and placed in the crook of Beth's arm.

Ryan could only think *this is a special moment. We should be sharing it together. Damn her, how could she have done this?*

Oddly enough there was no embarrassment between them, just a feeling of what might have been though neither would have admitted it to the other. The nurse guided Patrick and after a bit of fumbling he latched on.

'It's magic.'

'It's magic.'

They had spoken the words in unison and a startled look passed between them.

'This is a huge thing for the little man,' the nurse said after a little while. 'I think that's probably enough for now. His breathing is a bit laboured from the effort,' they both looked anxious 'but don't be too concerned. It's a big step for him and he's holding up very well. Let's put him back in the incubator now so he can rest and recover. I'm very pleased though.' She beamed at each of them in turn. 'Very pleased indeed.'

Ryan and Beth looked as if they

didn't know what to do next so the nurse suggested they go and get something to eat and come back in a couple of hours. They were happy to follow her directions, so completely were they out of their element. Seated opposite each other in the coffee shop and feeling much better for a good meal, the first proper one either had eaten in a long time, Beth expressed some regret at not being able to drink a toast to their new son.

'You don't need to worry,' Ryan said bitterly, 'I was drinking Guinness when you phoned me in Dublin. It's a shame I didn't realise at the time that I was the father of a newborn son.'

Beth felt as though she'd been struck. She jumped up without another word and ran from the room. There was no one other than Ryan to witness her headlong flight and he leapt from his chair instinctively to follow her. He stumbled over the leg and measured his length on the floor. *Just as well. If I'd caught her I'd have apologised and that*

I do not intend to do. I'm not the one to blame here. Ryan could tell himself as many times as he liked that he was the innocent victim but as he picked himself up and sat down again he couldn't help reflecting that there was an inescapable truth in what Beth had said to him. 'Didn't I have a right to know you were involved in a murder enquiry? Just how long were you going to keep your little secret? How do you think I felt hearing about that; hearing it from someone else?'

*   *   *

How do you tell the woman you love that you've been implicated in the murder of your niece and your brother-in-law? He'd wanted to. Once or twice he'd even begun to try but fear had pulled him up. What if she believed the rumours? Was it possible she could believe him capable of such a crime? He couldn't take the chance then and it was too late now. She'd heard not from him but from the lips of an accuser, or at the very least an innocent bystander who thought perhaps she ought to know. If the tables had been turned wouldn't he have followed her into hell and back? He thought so, but he hadn't been tested. She had been tested and found wanting; had failed to support him. But if he'd told her himself, would the outcome have been different? He'd never know. He would spend the rest of his life wondering what might have been. He snarled, an ugly look on his handsome face. The investigation wasn't over yet. For all he knew he'd spend the rest of his life behind bars wondering what might have been.

Useless to dwell on the past. What was done couldn't be undone. His pain was twofold. Beth was lost to him forever as the soulmate he'd known she could be; and their son, the little baby who even now was fighting for his life would, God willing he lived, would be the source of more pain as they wrestled over custody, over his future, over what would be best for him when, if things had been the way they should, he would have been the culmination of their love for each other. *Dammit, he is the culmination of our love for each other, even if that love has died.* But Ryan knew it hadn't. Not on his side, anyway.

He made his way slowly back to the care unit. He looked through the observation window. Beth was there already, holding her son; his son. She was so engrossed in what she was doing she didn't glance up, didn't see him at the window, wasn't watching as he turned away. Sadly he returned to the room they'd been allocated. He would try to get another couple of hours sleep. If he was still awake when she came back he would pretend. Tomorrow was going to be another long day.

18

Beth came exhausted to bed and looked across at where Ryan was gently snoring. She wasn't fooled for a moment. Even under the blanket she could see he was rigid — not the attitude at all of someone who was sleeping peacefully. *He doesn't even want to talk to me.* He had been wrong outside the nursery. Beth had been completely aware of his large frame watching her as she held their baby. No shadow had been thrown, no light diminished. It just seemed as if she always knew when he was around even if she couldn't see him. Her shoulders sagged as she sat on the bed. They'd enjoyed their meal together and just as they'd appeared to be getting along better he'd felled her with a single blow. He obviously had only contempt for her, for what she'd done. She'd killed his love. There was no going back. The only common ground they had now was Patrick and she could see the years of pain ahead of her as she watched the man she loved treating her like a stranger.

What about his work? What about his home? Would he expect them to take it in turns, for each to parent their child for a specified time then pass him back again like so much baggage? If Ryan returned to Dublin he wouldn't, she knew, stay away. He was his own boss and as far as she could tell at least comfortably off, if not more than. Siobhán, she knew, had gone home to pick up the reins. He'd told her that much while they were eating and apparently relaxed. If he could please himself as far as time was concerned he was in a position to make things even more difficult than they might otherwise be. Or maybe it would be easier. She didn't know and she had too much to worry about to think about it now. However had she got herself into this situation? *I fell in love, that's how. Deeply and forever with a man who now hates me.* She felt the bitterness rising to her throat.

Beth got into bed and fell into a deep and exhausted sleep filled with bad dreams. Ryan lay awake, letting his breathing return to normal. He had sensed her watching him, unable to release the tension from his body. He'd regretted his earlier outburst immediately. The poor girl was under enormous stress, they all were, and just as she had begun to unwind a bit he'd lashed out at her again. Small wonder she just wanted this to be a business arrangement. How can a child be a business arrangement?

Eventually Ryan drifted into troubled slumber and neither awoke refreshed. They would spend the coming hours in a state of fatigue. The only good thing was that they both now had got into phase with the clock and day was once more day and night, night.

★ ★ ★

Leaving breakfast in favour of seeing their son, they made their way together to the care unit. It seemed they weren't the only ones who hadn't had a good night. As they looked through the glass both could see Patrick's colour was not good. The nurse on the other side of the barrier raised her eyes to look at them. She shook her head slightly and gestured that she would come out to see them. The blood drained from Beth's face leaving her as pale as the sheet on which her tiny bundle was struggling for his life. Ryan and Beth moved as one towards the door and met the nurse on the threshold.

'What's wrong? What's the matter? Is he going to be okay?'

'Let's not stand in the corridor, Beth. I'd like you and Ryan to come to the waiting area with me so we can sit and talk.'

They walked quickly, anxious for news, whatever it was, and wanting to hear it as soon as possible. The nurse sat down with them which put fear into Beth's heart. *Aren't they usually a bit more formal than that?*

'As you could probably see, Patrick has taken a turn for the worse overnight. He's not in imminent danger but we do think he could do with a bit more help. We've increased the oxygen level in the incubator and we're going to go back to tube feeding. Nappy changing and anything else that is necessary will be done via the hand access.'

'Was it our fault? Because we took him out yesterday; cuddled him?'

She smiled sympathetically at this huge man who was going to pieces before her eyes. 'Of course not, Ryan. For a start it would have been entirely irresponsible on our part to allow that to happen if we didn't think he was up to it; and secondly, in spite of what he's going through now, it probably did him good to be held. It would have reassured him.'

Small comfort in the circumstances.

'Is there anything we can do?' Ryan asked.

'Be here for him. Support each other.' If she noticed the look that flickered between them she certainly didn't comment. 'We're still optimistic; it's just going to take a while. I'm not suggesting that you carry on as any normal visitor and come to see him once a day, Ryan. That would be silly and I rather think we'll be encouraging you to take time off rather than prompting you to visit. No, when you're here, sit with him; put your hands into the incubator as you were before, both of you. Your touch will be all important. The bond between you could be significant to his recovery.'

'Thank you, Nurse. We'll do whatever you say.'

'I'm relying on that, Ryan, which is why I'm suggesting now you go and have the breakfast which I'm as sure as I can be that you've missed. Come straight back afterwards and spend some time with Patrick.' She paused and looked directly from one to the other. 'Then I would suggest you go back to bed, Beth. The midwife will want to see you and in any case you need to build up your strength. It's not very long since you gave birth. We've got your mobile number if we need you, Ryan, and I know you won't be going very far.'

'But I don't . . . '

The nurse's raised eyebrow stopped Beth in mid-sentence. 'Quite. You know you can visit Patrick whenever you like. I can't stop you and I wouldn't distress you by trying. What I will do is emphasise that you will be no good to him when the time comes for you to feed him again if you're too tired to hold your head up.'

She stood up. The interview was over. 'Off with you then. Go and get that breakfast.'

★ ★ ★

There was none of the camaraderie during this meal that had been there the evening before. They sat looking bleakly at each other across the table. Ryan almost put his hand out to cover hers until he remembered she wanted nothing to do with him. She'd noticed the beginning of the gesture, the hurried withdrawal. *He can't even bear to touch me.* Neither had any appetite but forced down some toast and coffee, more intimidated by the nurse than either would have admitted.

'We'd better decide what we're going to do. When do you have to get back to Dublin?'

'There's no way I'm leaving, Beth.' He spoke so sharply she was startled.

'Ryan, I'm not trying to get rid of you. Can we call a truce? Please. At the moment Patrick's wellbeing is far more important than the sensibilities of either of us. You heard what the nurse said about touching him; bonding with him. If you told me you had to go now I would do everything in my power to make you stay. Our son needs us both.'

'I'm sorry, Beth. I thought . . . well, you know what I thought.' *Why do I have to keep saying the wrong thing? She didn't ask for me to jump down her throat like that.*

'Anyway, how do you feel about this? We could see him at different times of course but I think it might be better if we come together.' *If you can bear to spend the time with me, that is.* It was an afterthought she left unspoken. 'There are two hand holes. We could sit together, one each. I know you want to have as little as possible to do with me, Ryan, but under the circumstances I think Patrick's needs should come first and this way at least we'd be building a bond as an albeit reluctant family.'

Ryan dropped his eyes for fear of her seeing what they might say. He groaned inwardly. Hours spent in her company, inches away from her and not able to tell her how he felt. Would he be able to cope; to keep his inner self hidden from view? He had to cope. His son was depending on them. Under control now, he hoped, he raised his eyes and faced her square on.

'I agree. I think you're right. Obviously Patrick must come first.' It came out rather sharply.

Doesn't he know how cutting that sounds? Surely I don't deserve that. Doesn't he realise I'm only thinking about Patrick now? Beth was devastated at Ryan's apparent lack of understanding. 'I'm going to have to get back to the hotel to get some clean clothes. Siobhán left my overnight bag there. I don't have much but I feel as if I've been living in what I'm wearing for days.' He smiled; a beautiful sight. 'Come to think of it, I have. I can buy a few things as well. I don't need much. There's bound to be a laundry service at the hotel. Why don't we go and see Patrick now? Then I'll get a cab and we can meet back here later.'

'That's a good idea. And I'll phone and give Howard an update. I've texted him but he must be anxious to know what's going on.'

Howard. The last remnants of Ryan's smile fled as if they'd never been.

★ ★ ★

Ryan and Beth sat uncomfortably close together, necessitated by the proximity of the openings in Patrick's incubator. Neither had a clue as to how the other was feeling but each suffered the same upsurge of heat, intensified for both of them because it was almost impossible for them to sit side by side without touching.

Beth had to wonder about the effect Ryan had on her. She felt like a teenager experiencing her first crush. What wouldn't she have given then to be crushed in his arms? Powerless to stop these runaway thoughts Beth concentrated on Patrick. Was it her imagination, or had his colour improved slightly? She decided it was just wishful thinking stroked his tiny arm and the back of his hand with one finger.

Ryan had his own reflections. *She's like an earth mother; the proud giver of life to this small child. I was just a tool to facilitate the miracle.* The association sent heat to his loins and he could only be grateful that he was sitting down and his automatic reaction was hidden from view. The pain was unbelievable but he wouldn't have wanted to forego it even if he'd been able.

But he wasn't just a tool. He knew that. It was as real to her then as it was to him. He was sure of that. Except, what was it she'd called it, the romance of a cruise. Ryan had shunned the company of women since he'd returned from the *Mediterranean Adventurer*, at least in so far as any sexual liaison was concerned. His celibacy had been of choice and he hadn't felt any of the need that was so much a part of his life before. He hadn't wanted to touch another woman while he still loved Beth; and here she was, sitting next to him, thigh to thigh, knee to knee, and all at once the craving was there again.

His hand where it rested on his son's upper arm was, he realised, barely an inch from hers. The urge to move it and lay it over hers was impelling.

He withdrew and made an excuse about needing to blow his nose. He rushed from the care unit and stood outside looking in, elaborately taking out his hankie and going through the expected motion. *This is definitely not going to be easy.* Ryan pointed to his watch and gestured to Beth. She nodded, blew an air kiss from her hand to her son and joined him in the corridor.

'Maybe we should be going, if it's okay with you,' he said.

'I'd like to stay with him a bit longer but it made sense, what the nurse said. I don't like to admit it but truthfully I am shattered. Unless you'd rather not we can meet in the coffee shop later; have something to eat before we go and see Patrick again.' She knew it was asking for trouble, but she didn't like eating alone and didn't suppose he did either.

'Can you text me maybe when you're ready?'

'Yes, that's fine. Meanwhile I'll go and get a shower and some clean clothes.'

Beth went to the nurses' station to let them know they were leaving the unit and to double check they had the right number for Ryan. Then she followed instructions and went back to the room she and Ryan had recently vacated to await a visit from the midwife. Ryan stepped out into the early spring sunshine, picked up a taxi and headed for his hotel.

19

Beth had intended making a couple of phone calls but the next thing she knew was a hand on her shoulder, the midwife waking her gently to check her over. She'd been asleep for over an hour.

'You're getting along fine. I'll come and see you again tomorrow morning but you can ask for me at any time. I understand they'll be moving you to another floor where there are facilities for long-stay visitors.' Seeing that Beth was looking slightly startled, she added quickly, 'It's perfectly normal, if a baby needs long-term care or a mother wants to stay on the premises to be near her child. Don't worry about it. You shouldn't need any special postnatal care but the less running around you do the better. You'll be more comfortable there; be able to make yourself a drink;

have a bath. Not exactly home from home but not quite like a hospital room either.'

'Thank you. I'm very grateful.'

'You're very welcome.' She breezed out of the room.

Fully awake now, Beth phoned her mother. She'd only spoken to her very briefly shortly after Patrick was born, trying to reassure her when she was terrified herself.

'No, Mum, don't come yet,' she'd said. 'The baby's poorly and I don't think he can have visitors. He'll be all right, I'm sure. I'll call you again as soon as I can.'

Beth felt guilty. *Poor Mum. She and Dad must be frantic. That was the day before yesterday and I've only punched off a couple of hurried texts since.*

'Mum, it's Beth.'

'Thank goodness. Your father and I have been beside ourselves. How are you? How is the baby?'

'I'm fine, Mum. They're really looking after me well. Patrick's not — '

'Patrick? You've called him Patrick.'

'Yes, well he's not too great, I'm afraid. They're keeping him in an incubator; something to do with his lungs not being fully formed and not working properly yet.'

'Oh my goodness! Is he going to be okay?'

'They say they're confident that with time everything will be as it should be. In the meantime I'm staying here at the hospital. Did I tell you they'd moved us to the Radcliffe?'

'Oh Beth. Are we allowed to come? We want to see you; both of you. We can be there in an hour.'

'Yes, Mum, of course you can come, but it would be better if you left it till this evening I think. He's in the infant care unit. Text me when you get here and I'll come down to get you.'

Beth was anxious about what would happen if they came straight up themselves and found Ryan with her. After all, they weren't aware of all the facts.

'No, don't worry. We'll find our way. We can't wait to see you both.'

Not worth making an issue of, so she didn't. Beth's next call was to the office where she spoke first to Howard and then Simon.

'We're okay, Howard . . . No, he's not bullying me . . . Yes, of course I'll be coming back to the flat if that's all right with you. They're keeping me in for a while; for observation and to be near Patrick . . . Not tonight; my parents are coming but if you can make it tomorrow that would be great. Is Simon free? Can I have a word? See you tomorrow then.'

'Beth?'

'Hello, Simon. I'm so sorry to have disappeared like that. There wasn't time to tell you, it all happened so quickly . . . Yes, of course I am . . . No, I'd tell you, wouldn't I? Or Howard would. Thank heaven for Howard; I don't know what I'd have done without him . . . In a few days would be lovely. Love to Linda. Bye.'

She was just thinking of lying down again when she received Ryan's text. 'On my way. With you in ten.'

★　★　★

Ryan was already sitting at a table in the corner when Beth walked into the coffee shop. *My goodness, he scrubs up well. It's just not fair.* Wearing a bright white sweatshirt which did nothing to hide the muscles beneath, and with his unruly hair for once combed neatly into place, Ryan looked like any woman's dream of tall, dark and handsome. He looked up as she approached and might have stood as an advert for a toothpaste brand leader but, more importantly, she could see his teeth because he was smiling at her.

'You look much better. Did you have a good sleep?'

Did that mean I was a complete mess before? Stop it, Beth, he's handing you an olive branch here. Have the grace and the sense to accept it. She smiled back at him.

'I think I was asleep before my head hit the pillow. I could have cried when the midwife woke me up but she's checked me out and everything seems to be okay, as far as I'm concerned that is. Oh, by the way, they're moving me to another floor, somewhere people stay when they have a relative in hospital. You won't be able to sleep with me anymore.' For goodness sake, where did that come from? Fortunately Ryan was in a mood to be amused.

'I think you already told me that months ago.' But he wasn't angry. She rather suspected he was enjoying her discomfiture.

'I spoke to my boss. He's happy for me to take as long as I need.' This time she had the sense not to mention Howard. 'And I phoned my parents. They've been worried sick. I guess my quick call when I was waiting for you to arrive the other day was a bit cruel but I was so worried, I wasn't thinking about how they would feel. Anyway, they'll be here later to see their grandson.'

Ryan raised an eyebrow, throwing her once more into confusion.

'I didn't ask. I'm sorry. Your parents — are they still . . . ?'

'Alive and well and living an hour's drive from Dublin. No, Beth, I haven't told them yet.' Ryan was amused at her discomfiture. *She just doesn't realise how beautiful she is when she looks confused or embarrassed at saying the wrong thing.* 'Don't worry. Everything happened so quickly and I don't want to drag them over here until Patrick's better. After losing one granddaughter and one expected grandchild it would break their hearts if . . . oh, Beth, I'm so sorry.' She'd suddenly gone grey. 'I didn't mean to upset you. I'm convinced he's going to make it. He's only gorgeous; he couldn't have been born not to pull through.'

This time Ryan did put his hand over Beth's. This time he didn't draw back, and neither did she. There was a long pause where each wondered but neither would meet the other's eyes.

'Well, if your parents are coming we'd better get some food down us; gird our loins.' *Oh, God in heaven, now I'm doing it!* 'Do they know about me?'

'Only that we're not together. I haven't told them anything about what happened.'

'What did happen, Beth?'

Suddenly conversation was finished and they ordered and ate in silence.

★　★　★

There was no discernible change in Patrick when they returned to the unit. They sat side by side again, each with a hand on their son. As before their thighs, arms and shoulders abutted but this time they were so out of tune neither felt the rush of desire that usually accompanied even the slightest physical contact. They sat for the most part without speaking, only breaking into the stillness from time to time to comment on the baby. Though she knew it was necessary, Beth was terribly distressed to see all the equipment that was wired up, particularly hating the tube in his tiny little nose.

'It must be so uncomfortable for him with that thing in his nostril,' Ryan said.

She turned towards him and found that Ryan's eyes had suddenly filled with tears. *I didn't appreciate he felt it as much as I do, she realised. But of course he does. Patrick's just as much his child as mine.* For a moment she softened, until she remembered the bitterness in his voice when he'd asked, 'What did happen, Beth?' He might have a lot of tender feelings, but none of them were directed at her. He hadn't forgiven her. He'd never forgive her. She focussed again on her son.

A while later she looked up to see Howard standing outside at the observation window. She rushed out to see him. He gave her a huge bear hug that was not lost on Ryan. He ground his teeth.

'Beth, it's so good to see you. Everyone sends their love. How is the little chap?'

'Not great, Howard, and I'm not allowed to take you inside the unit but at least you can see him from here.'

'Well at least he's hanging on in there. I know you told me not to come today but I've brought some more of your things. I didn't think the few bits I brought before would be enough. I hope you don't mind, I raided your room at the flat; took some of the stuff you were wearing when you were first pregnant. I thought you might not be able to get into your size 8s yet.'

Beth wondered how many men would even have known her dress size. 'Howard, you are a star. You're wasted, you know.' An unreadable look flickered across his face. 'No, I didn't mean . . . you know I didn't. It's just that you do caring so well.'

'Giving you a hard time is he, Ryan?'

'Just a bit.'

'I had a card, you know. From Jasper.'

'You what?'

'Just a few words. Nothing to indicate that he's changed his mind but a complete turnaround from not wanting his mum and dad even to let me know where he is. Thing is, I'm not sure how I feel.'

'Is there an address? Can you contact him?'

'No, but I can always send something through his parents. He'd know that. Anyway, that's enough about me for now. Let's have another look at your beautiful baby then I'll get out of your way and leave you to it.'

He left her with another hug and a kiss on both cheeks, as much to needle Ryan as a sign of his affection for her. It didn't go unnoticed. Beth returned to Ryan.

'Do you want to stretch your legs? You've been sitting here for well over an hour now.'

'Good idea.' He walked off. He didn't invite her to go with him. She picked up the bag that Howard had left in the corridor and went to find out about her new accommodation.

* * *

It took Beth some time to get herself sorted, and she used the opportunity of washing her hair and having a long soak in the bath which soothed her aching body but not her bruised feelings. Physically refreshed at least, she put on clean trousers and a loose top, not actually designed for pregnancy but perfect in the circumstances, and silently blessed Howard again for his care and his taste. At least she'd be able to face her parents looking as if she was a member of the human race and not the zombie she'd begun to feel like.

Not wanting them to arrive and find an unexplained Ryan with Patrick, she headed for the coffee shop for a quick snack, half expecting to find him there.

She was grateful that he wasn't; she didn't fancy another meal in cold silence. And if he'd been sitting at one of the tables, how could she not have joined him? *I guess this is going to get worse before it gets better — if it gets better.*

Ryan was with Patrick when she got back to the care unit. She took her place beside him and tried again. 'How is he, do you think? Any change?'

'It's so hard to tell. The paediatrician came by a while ago but she didn't have anything to add.' Beth was mortified she'd missed her and it showed. 'Don't worry, I told her you were having a much needed break.'

'Thank you, that was kind of you. Have you been here long?'

'Most of the time. I went for a walk as you suggested, but as I don't know the area around the hospital and I didn't want to get lost it seemed more sensible to walk the corridors. That was totally uninspiring so I came back fairly quickly. Been here ever since.'

'You must be hungry. I've just had something myself. I can keep an eye on him if you want to have a bite to eat.'

'No appetite. I'll grab a late snack when I get back to the hotel.'

She thought he looked tired. It didn't stop him from still being the most gorgeous thing she'd ever seen on two legs.

'I expect my pare — '

And there they were, outside peering in. Beth and Ryan both went out to meet them. After the initial hugs and checking their daughter over to make sure she was okay, they both looked at the man standing slightly to the back and to one side; a man they'd never met. They had expected Howard.

'Mum, Dad, this is Ryan, Patrick's father. Ryan . . . Rosemary and David.'

'Sure I'm delighted to meet you both, and only sorry it's at such a worrying time for us all. He's a beautiful boy though, your grandson, and putting up a great fight. Would you just look at him?'

Beth was amazed. How can he just turn on the charm like that? *He's so . . . Irish. He should smile more often. It suits him better than the grim look he's been carrying lately. Oh look, he's won Mum over already.*

Rosemary cast an arch look at her daughter as Ryan continued to flirt with them all. Beth was going to have a hard time explaining this. He didn't appear to be the rogue who had left her to finish her pregnancy on her own, an assumption which she was sure her mother had made and which she hadn't made any effort to correct. Would he tell them it was she who'd chucked him, not the other way round? She didn't even bother to wonder how she'd explain that one away. She was just grateful they were getting on so well and rather touched as Ryan pointed out Patrick's features to them, remarking on his eyelashes which even at this tender age promised to be as dark and thick as his father's.

'Did you have far to come, David?'

'About an hour's drive. Fortunately it's a nice evening.'

'The hospital café is quite nice. Would you like to have a coffee before you go home; set you up for the journey?'

'An excellent idea. Lead on, young man.'

Damn him, he's pulling the ground out from under my feet. Ryan took her mother's arm and Beth followed lamely behind with her father who came straight to the point, albeit speaking quietly thank goodness.

'He's nice, Beth. Why aren't you together?'

'Not now, Dad, he'll hear us. I'll talk to you about it another time.' And with that David had to be content. Beth knew she wouldn't be able to put him off indefinitely, and certainly not her mother, but there was no way she could cope with this added trauma at the moment. They sat, Rosemary and David on one side of the table, Beth and Ryan on the other. Beth explained as best she could with her own incomplete understanding just what the problems were that Patrick was dealing with.

'But he'll be all right, won't he?' Rosemary asked.

'We're trying not to get our hopes up too much but they seem very positive although of course they won't commit themselves. I think he looks a bit better this evening. What do you think, Ryan?'

He slid his arm along the back of her chair and rested his hand on her shoulder. He was toying with her; appreciating this most awkward situation she found herself in. She kicked him under the table.

'Sure I think you're right.'

He's exaggerating his accent! He must know what effect his burr has on women and my mother is no different from any other woman. He reached down to rub his ankle where she'd made contact. To do so of course he had to lean in towards Beth. *Damn him*, she thought. *He's enjoying every moment of this. Just wait till I get him alone.*

'The fact that we can touch him helps us and they've assured us it's good for him too. And it helps us all to bond.'

He is so playing this! At least what he's saying is true. I know he wouldn't amuse himself at Patrick's expense. Beth kept her reflections to herself.

'I'm staying at a nearby hotel and they're keeping Beth in for a while. Obviously she needs looking after as well.' He turned his head towards her and hugged her shoulders, smiling as if butter wouldn't melt in his mouth.

'We can sit with the baby any time we like; there are no restrictions on visiting. Unfortunately we've only each been able to hold him once so we're praying he'll be able to breast feed soon — ' Beth kicked him again. ' — even if they only take him out for a short time. We'll let you know if there are any changes of course, and you're welcome to come at any time — if, that is, you don't mind sitting on the outside looking in.'

Beth was indignant. The cheek of the man! *Who does he think he is? Patrick's father, that's who.*

Ryan's phone rang. He looked at the number. It was Siobhán.

'I'm so sorry. Please excuse me, I have to take this call.' And he *was* sorry. He'd been thoroughly enjoying himself.

'Ryan, it's Siobhán. You have to come home. They've set a date for the hearing.'

20

Ryan was stunned. Of course he knew it was coming at some time, but he'd had no indication as to when. He moved away from the table.

'I'm a bit tied up at the moment, sis. Can I call you back in about half an hour? We can have a proper discussion. Great. Thanks. Later then.'

As he moved to join them Rosemary and David were standing up. 'I think we'd better be on our way. We'll come back again soon. Good to meet you, Ryan.'

David and Ryan shook hands vigorously. Ryan kissed Rosemary on the cheek. She actually blushed. They turned to say goodbye to Beth.

'Don't worry, sweetheart, we'll find our own way out.'

'Okay, Mum. See you soon.'

'Shall we go and say goodnight to

Patrick? Then I'll be off too.'

It's all very well for him to make a show while Mum and Dad were here, but he can't bear to be with me now they've gone. Beth was sad. She didn't bother to say all the things she'd been storing up about him putting his arm round her and pretending to her parents that everything was okay. There didn't seem to be much point. They went into the care unit and each put a hand in to touch their son. Neither was prepared just to wave at him from the window. They left together, Beth to go to her room and Ryan to make an urgent phone call, though he didn't tell her that of course.

'What have they said, Siobhán? When's the hearing?'

'A week today. There's an envelope here addressed to you, identical to the one my notification came in. Do you want me to open it?'

'Please.' He waited while she read the contents.

'Yes, it's the same. It doesn't give any

details other than summoning you to the meeting on 26th March. It isn't a request, it's an order, but so is mine so there's nothing we can read into it other than we have to be there. How's Patrick?'

'Holding his own, but it's so difficult to tell if there's any improvement. I'm not sure they know either. I'm going to hang on here for as long as I can, sis. Another week could make all the difference to him and I don't want to leave him until I absolutely have to, whatever happens.'

'No, I understand, of course. I wouldn't call you back now if I had any choice.'

'What about you? Are you holding up okay? Is everything all right at work? I'm sure you're more than capable of holding the fort.'

Lots of quick-fire questions and answers back and forth, but there was little either could do to help the other at this stage.

'I'll keep in touch, Siobhán. I can't

tell you how much I appreciate you being there. Bye now.'

'Bye, Ryan. Take care. Give my love to Beth.'

He didn't answer. Instead he switched off his phone and made his way back to the hotel. Somehow he'd lost his appetite. He helped himself to a strong drink from the mini-bar, kicked off his shoes and lay on the bed with hands folded behind his head, moving only to take the occasional sip from his glass or, on one occasion, to top it up. He gave himself over to reflection. *I knew it had to come sooner or later. At least they haven't arrested me yet, but I don't suppose that means they won't do so after the hearing. Surely I can't have found Patrick only to lose him now, not because of his struggle to survive but because I might be behind bars for the whole of his childhood?* The lump in his throat felt the size of a football. He reached again for the glass.

★   ★   ★

Time seemed to take on different and differing properties over the next few days. Seeming hours spent sitting with Patrick turned out to be only one or two at the most. A short spell at his side they found out later was actually nearly four hours. Though Beth and Ryan snatched many of their meals together, keeping to their practice of sharing rather than dividing the moments spent with their son, conversation was desultory. They regained neither intimacy nor animosity; just two people side by side willing their child to live, to fight, to prevail. Beth rushed into the care unit one afternoon.

'Sorry I'm late. The midwife came to see me just as I was leaving.'

'You okay?'

'Everything is as it should be. It just held me up, that's all. I have a horrible feeling they might send me home soon if it looks like Patrick's stay is going to stretch into weeks. I'm not sure how long I'm allowed to be here.'

'Beth, what do you think? Do you

think he looks at bit more — I'm not quite sure how to put it — natural maybe? Like he's doing it on his own, although I know he isn't; you can see everything is still wired up.'

This was the first time she'd heard him with anything like animation in his voice for a long time. She didn't know he was watching the days rush by and that soon he'd have to leave. Although when she looked at Patrick she became excited as well.

'I think you might be right. Oh, Ryan, do you think he could be turning the corner?'

'Let's not get too worked up.' Though neither of them could help it. 'You stay here while I go and get the nurse.'

Nurse came and then went to get Staff Nurse. 'I agree he's looking better. While I'm here why don't we try taking him out for a few minutes? Put him to the breast maybe. See if he can remember how from before.'

Beth was desperate to feed him

herself and anxious to stop the tedium of expressing her milk. There was a nursing chair in the corner of the unit and she settled herself into it while the staff nurse detached Patrick from his support system and brought him over to his mother. Ryan watched as he struggled at first, his tiny hands flailing around as they sought and then found his mother's soft flesh. Instinct is an amazing thing. Patrick suckled away happily, dropping off only once. Beth put a finger on either side of her nipple and guided him back. His father, overcome with an emotion he didn't quite know how to deal with, dropped to his knees sideways on and supported Beth's arm and thus the baby's head with his huge hand. Tears spilled shamelessly as he watched this miracle that was the continuation of life, every species having its own way of nurturing its young.

I don't know how I'm going to be able to leave him. How can I tell her I've got to go? Maybe she'll just be glad to be rid of me at last. At least if I know he's on the mend, if he's not critical, it won't be so bad. What if they arrest me? What if I never see Patrick again?

Ryan's tears of joy turned to tears of despair. Luckily Beth didn't know the difference.

'We don't want to overtire him, do we?' Staff Nurse's voice broke into his thoughts. 'We should give him a rest now. Perhaps you'd like to carry him back to the incubator, Ryan?' And once more he held the living breathing wonder that was his son.

★   ★   ★

The next couple of days flew by. Patrick still wasn't well enough to dispense with the incubator, but the improvement was discernible and Beth's joy at being at last able to feed him herself was so strong you could almost touch it. Two things happened in parallel. Beth was told she could extend her stay at the hospital. Now that he was breastfeeding Patrick needed her often. It would have been completely impractical for her to commute. Though the town where she lived wasn't far from Oxford, the journey both ways would nonetheless take up most of the time between feeds and she would have been exhausted. The other thing was Ryan telling her of his impending departure.

'I have to go back to Dublin for a while, Beth. Now Patrick's out of danger I'll be leaving tomorrow.'

Beth felt it like a blow to her centre of gravity. Most of the time they'd spent together the last few days they'd displayed indifference to each other. Except when her mum and dad came to visit, she'd realised. He managed to maintain the façade of happy families while they were there. When Howard came he got the hump. He's only stayed because of Patrick. *Now that he's out of danger, relatively speaking, he can't wait to leave me.*

She knew that she was being irrational. She knew also that she was completely and irrevocably in love with this giant of a man who had displayed such a tender side, no matter what else he might have done; well, not exactly no matter but it didn't stop her being hopelessly attached to the man who was the father of her child. Pride was her saviour. Pride helped hide the true nature of her feelings for him.

'I'm glad you could stay long enough to see him on the mend. Will you be able to come back soon?'

The answer was so important to her but she managed to put the question in a conversational tone without betraying her anxiety. She might have been asking Simon or Claire.

'I'm hoping so, Beth. There's something I have to deal with at home but I'll be back as soon as I can. If it's okay with you I'll text or phone to find out how he's doing. Obviously I'd rather hear it from you than from one of the nurses.'

At least I'm one point ahead of the nurses in his estimation.

'Will you be in to see him before you leave?'

'I'll come in on my way to the airport. About half ten. Shall we go and have our last meal together in the coffee shop before I go back to the hotel?'

It sounded to Beth like the Last Supper. They made it last as long as they could, though neither realised what the other was doing.

I suppose eating with me is just a touch better than eating on her own. She doesn't have a clue how I feel about her. She mustn't *have a clue how I feel about her.*

Oh the misunderstandings that keep two people apart. After going back to say goodnight to Patrick, Ryan left. Beth saw him for only a few minutes the next morning when he came to say goodbye. Her heart was breaking. So was his.

21

Siobhán was waiting for Ryan as he came out of the terminal. His first thought was how well she looked. Obviously being busy was doing her good. He also noted the tiny worry lines in the corners of her eyes. There was a lot riding on this hearing, both regarding the evidence, if there was any, that someone had planned to murder her husband and, by association, Siobhán herself, and the involvement or otherwise of her brother.

Parked in a restricted area she nevertheless jumped out of the car as soon as she saw him and the intensity of their hug was evidence of how pent up they both were.

'It seems like an age since I last saw you. How's the baby?'

'It looks like he's going to make it. The last few days have been remarkable. It broke my heart to leave him.'

'And Beth?'

'She's okay, I think. Much better now that she can feed Patrick herself and see him getting better all the time.'

'No, Ryan, I meant did it break your heart to leave her too?'

'What sort of a question is that for a sister to be asking her brother?'

'A concerned one. If you don't confide in me who else do you have to talk to?'

They got into the car, Ryan in the driver's seat, and set off for home. He sat in silence for a while, negotiating the traffic as he made his way out of the airport. She kept quiet until they got on to the open road and was rewarded for her discretion when he heaved a huge sigh and began to open up.

'What can I do, Siobhán? She doesn't want me.'

'Are you sure?'

'She's made it abundantly clear. As Patrick's father she's willing to include me in her life for his sake, but whatever feelings she had for me disappeared in the wake of that ship.'

She asked again, 'Are you sure?'

'I tried, when her parents came to visit, to act as if we were a unit, the three of us, and she resented it like hell. No, Siobhán, I'm sure. I'm allowed to be Patrick's father; she even asked if I knew when I'd be back. But as far as she's concerned she wants nothing to do with me.'

'If you're right, and I'm not convinced you are, the first thing we must do is get this hearing out of the way. After that you need to go back to Oxford and establish the boundaries and a strategy of how you plan to raise your child. It's not going to be easy with you living in another country.'

'And with her living with Howard.'

Ryan had no inkling of his sister's thoughts. Some men are so blind. Siobhán didn't think it was for her to point out Howard's sexual orientation. If Beth had wanted Ryan to know she'd have told him. In the meantime, presumably she had her reasons for the deception. She'd have given quite a lot for a one to one with Beth but until the hearing was over there was nothing she could do. Nothing any of them could do.

'Does she know why you've come home?'

'Absolutely not! As far as she knows I had some business to attend to. What am I going to do if they find me guilty, Siobhán? What if they lock me up? How long will it be before I can see my son? How long before I can see either of them? No, sis, I didn't tell her.'

They made it home in good time and spent the early part of the evening sorting out their clothes for next day's hearing. Ryan took first one suit then another out of his wardrobe, decided the grey made less of a statement than the navy, or at least a less obvious on, (though Beth would have preferred the latter had she been able to see), and set it to one side. The shirt and tie were also chosen for their discretion, after which he just became irritated with himself. *What bloody difference how I'm dressed? Either I'm a condemned man or I'm not.*

Siobhán also chose her outfit with care. It was a long time since she'd been widowed and lost her children. She still grieved; she always would; but she'd given up wearing mourning clothes. Tomorrow, though, it would be more appropriate for her to be seen in something subdued, in keeping with the matter in hand. She feared for Ryan, not because she believed there would be a shred of evidence against him but because she didn't understand the workings of the court. Could they pin this awful deed on him? Has there even been an awful deed or was it just a tragic accident? The next twenty-four hours would bring the answer.

Clothes laid out ready, they met back in the lounge.

'I feel like getting drunk.'

'That would certainly create a good impression, going into court smelling of alcohol.'

'I said I felt like it, not that I was going to.'

'A good meal would be better for both of us. I cooked a stew. I'm going to warm it up now and you will do me the courtesy, please, of at least pretending to enjoy it.'

'No problem there. I love your stews.' But he knew what she meant. He had no appetite and he was pretty sure she didn't either. They went through the motions, allowing themselves one glass of wine each, just for a bit of Dutch courage. They would both need a clear head the next day.

They sat in the lounge and watched a DVD — *When Harry Met Sally*. Not a great choice. It was too close to home. Can't live with each other, can't live without each other, but that was only on his side. Beth had made it quite obvious that she could live without him; had done so for months until she felt she had no choice but to tell him of his son's existence. Unlike the film, though, he couldn't foresee a happy ending.

Ryan and Siobhán stayed up as long as they could, neither expecting to sleep, both preferring company to staring at the bedroom ceiling for half the night. Eventually they gave in. The ceilings in both their rooms got a lot of attention in the next few hours. Coffee was all either of them could manage in the morning and they drove silently to the courthouse to meet their fate.

Neither brother nor sister had ever had any reason to go to court before now but they'd been briefed on what to expect. Someone showed them to their seats. It wasn't a large chamber. While they waited for proceedings to begin Siobhán fiddled with her hair and Ryan picked at his fingernails. Officials entered and the court rose.

'Good luck, Ryan. I believe in you, whatever happens.' She squeezed his hand.

In spite of their lack of knowledge of procedure it was all over so quickly they could hardly believe it had taken place at all, except now they had a result

— of sorts. All present were thanked for attending and given the following information:

An investigation had proved the car brakes were tampered with. Forensics found evidence of a set of fingerprints. However, the prints were not on any database. Other fingerprints belonging to members of the family were found all over the vehicle, but none were found on the tampered brakes. Until such time as the owner of the incriminating prints could be traced, the court declared an open verdict. Commiserations were offered to the widow. Court was dismissed.

Siobhán and Ryan stumbled out of the courtroom. Sitting in the car, she couldn't understand why he looked so grave. 'What is it, Ryan? What's the matter? It's over. At last it's over.'

'It's not over, Siobhán. Don't you see? Until they find out whose prints were on the brakes I'm still a suspect. Oh, I know they didn't say as much in so many words but the implication, at least to me, was that I could have wiped my prints or worn gloves. Finding another set doesn't clear me, Siobhán. I won't be free until they find the bastard who did this. They might as well have found nothing; my name still isn't cleared.'

'You're wrong, Ryan. You must be wrong. How could they let you go free if you were still under suspicion?'

'I've been under suspicion ever since it happened, sis. Nothing's changed just because they don't have any evidence against me. Nothing.'

The only time she'd ever seen him looking so bleak was when Beth had finished their relationship so abruptly last year.

'I've been waiting for the hearing, Siobhán; expecting to be exonerated. After all, I know I'm innocent. I was going to tell her, couldn't wait to tell her how wrong she'd been, to beg if necessary to have as much to do with Patrick's upbringing as her. I can't do that now. I can't let my son grow up knowing his father is suspected of a crime of the worst possible kind; and he will know. You can bet your bottom dollar someone will tell him. I have to pull back, Siobhán. I have to let them go. I have to let them both go. Oh God, what am I going to do?'

For the first time since they were children Siobhán saw her brother weep; agonised sobs wrenched themselves from his body and he kept repeating, over and over, 'What am I going to do? Whatever am I going to do?'

* * *

Can't he pick up a phone? Doesn't he even want to know how Patrick is? Beth hadn't heard from Ryan since he'd left two days before. She was finding it so difficult to come to terms with his not being there. In spite of the awkwardness between them the intimacies they'd shared over their baby, the hushed interchanges when they discussed his progress, had all become part of her daily routine. Even the sometimes atmospherically cold meals they ate together were better than the isolation she was going through now. She missed him so much it hurt, and to the hurt she now added anger.

It may be out of sight out of mind as far as I'm concerned, but he had no business asking if he could contact me about Patrick and then maintaining this . . . this silence. Beth wanted to be able to tell Ryan that their son was making good progress; the paediatrician had used the adjective so she hadn't made it up. It would be a little while before she'd be able to take him home but each day he spent more time out of the incubator, more time in her arms. She'd been allowed to change his nappy; to bathe him; all under the careful eye of a nurse but all in preparation for when she left the hospital.

Her parents had come yesterday. They'd asked where Ryan was. He'd become their blue-eyed boy, that was for sure. Except he didn't have blue eyes. His eyes were brown pools she wanted to drown in. Even without him being there, her body was being reclaimed by its old feelings and desire rose in her unchecked. She could only be grateful her eagerness was invisible to her mum and dad.

'He's had to go back to Dublin on business, Mum. I believe he'll be coming back soon, as soon as he can.'

'What a pity we've missed him. Do give him our love, won't you?'

I'd rather give him mine! Beth knew these thoughts were doing her no good at all but she was helpless to control them. It was ridiculous how much she needed him, even though they spent a lot of time arguing when they were together. It reminded her of that film, *When Harry Met Sally.* She was pondering the imponderables when her phone rang.

'Beth? Ryan. Sorry I didn't get in touch yesterday. I was away from home and there was a dodgy signal.'

Not the truth but, though he hated

telling lies, the truth was something he couldn't tell her at the moment. He had no idea if that moment would ever come.

'How's Patrick?'

'You wouldn't believe it, Ryan. I'm feeding him. I'm holding him. I even gave him a bath yesterday morning.'

So she'd been bathing their son while he was awaiting his fate in the courtroom. 'You'll be there for a while still, in the hospital?'

'Yes, he won't be ready to go home for a few days, if then. They haven't said. But he's definitely better. Why?'

'It's just that I can't get back at the moment. Give him a kiss for me, will you.' He took his courage in both hands. 'One for you too.'

'Bye.' *Dammit, he sends me a kiss and all I can say is 'bye'.*

Beth was kicking herself that she hadn't given him more encouragement. She hadn't even asked when she'd hear from him again.

Well that went down like a lead

balloon. *She didn't even acknowledge it.* Ryan was licking the wounds of what he felt was rejection. He'd be more careful next time.

22

'I've made up my mind, Siobhán. I know we decided you working in the family business wasn't a good idea, but you're doing such a good job without seeming to suffer any emotional angst that I want you to stay.' He paused. 'I want you to stay for the time being while I'm tripping backward and forward to Oxford. In spite of what she thinks, Beth needs my support while Patrick is so little. Yes, I know,' he said, responding to her raised eyebrow, 'Howard is on hand. But he's not Howard's son, he's my son, and I'm going to see him and I'm going to help her.'

Siobhán was overjoyed to see her strong, assertive brother back again. He'd been so broken up. There was nothing he could do about the court's decision; that was out of his hands. But at least he knew now where he stood. The Ryan she knew was going to take his life back into his own hands and do what he thought was right.

'It's taken me a long time to get this far, Ryan, but I'm enjoying it so much you're going to have to prise me away. I haven't told you but the nightmares have stopped. Maybe it's because I'm so tired there isn't room for bad dreams; maybe it's because I have something else to think about. But we're both moving forward. Of course I'll stay.'

'Just made sure you don't usurp my authority entirely, girl. I'll be back full time eventually.'

'Yes, and I think there might be room for expansion if we're both there. We could even think about the market in the Far East. Anyway, that's for the future. When are you going back to England?'

Tomorrow, if it's okay with you and if I can get a flight.'

'Suits me.'

'Right, I'll book a seat and then perhaps you'd allow me to take the prettiest woman in Dublin out for dinner tonight.'

'I'm not surprised women fall at your feet.' She rushed on before he could make any comment about one particular woman. 'You're full of it. Don't you come your wiles with me, Ryan Donovan. And yes, dinner's a great idea.'

'See? It works.' He beamed at her and ducked as she threw the tea towel at his head. 'I'll be off to book my ticket. Choose where you'd like to go and reserve a table if you don't mind.'

'Some escort you are. Now I even have to book my own table.'

Ryan made his arrangements and joined his sister for dinner looking crushingly handsome in a dark blue suit. Somewhere, somehow, he'd regained his confidence and ready humour kept them both suitably entertained throughout the meal.

'It's good to have you back, Ryan.'

'It's good to be back.'

'Have you decided what you're going to do? Exactly what you're going to do?'

He looked at her over the rim of his wine glass, a serious expression on his face but with the old sparkle back in his eye. 'I have that, Siobhán. I have that.'

'And that is?'

'I'm going to claim what's mine!'

His sister wasn't at all sure if he meant just his son or if he had another agenda, nor did she ask.

★   ★   ★

Beth was feeling neglected. She knew she had no right to expect anything from Ryan, but one call and a couple of quick texts — one asking about Patrick and the other saying he'd be over the next day — were all the communication she'd had. Okay, if he could be business like then so could she. In spite of her reasons for walking away from him and leaving a love few people are lucky enough ever to find, in spite of then keeping from him the knowledge of his impending fatherhood, the cat was now well and truly out of the bag. He was as much Patrick's parent as she was and had as much right to a say in his future. Not that she was quite ready to let him know that, but there was no way Ryan would back off now. She wouldn't herself. If Patrick had to grow up with his father's name under a cloud then so be it. Now they just had to learn how to tolerate each other without their son becoming aware of the animosity between them. Ryan would never forgive her for what she'd done; for either thing she'd done. She knew she'd made a terrible mistake last summer, then she'd compounded it.

It doesn't matter that I did it for the right reason. What kind of a person keeps a child from his father? It crossed her mind for a fleeting moment to apologise; to ask him to take her back. *Where is your pride, Beth? The man knows he's lucky to be rid of you. Why would he have you back now?* Since she couldn't think of any reason why he should, she waited in miserable loneliness.

'Good mornin' to you. I couldn't wait to see our boy again; managed to get a really early flight. How is he?'

A different Ryan had walked into the ward. *Oh my, he looks gorgeous.* Beth's chin dropped and she almost forgot to answer him. 'Well. He's doing really well.'

'I thought maybe he wouldn't be in the incubator. Hello, little man.' Ryan put his hand in and Patrick obligingly made a fist around his finger.

'It's hardly at all now. His progress, now it's begun, seems to be steaming ahead. They'll be in soon to get him out so I can feed him. It's like he can't get enough.'

'Isn't he the lucky one?'

She had the grace to blush. The Ryan she saw now was the Ryan she'd met on the ship. His eyes were alive with mischief; he was smiling; he was having fun, at her expense. That's what it was, she realised. He was having fun. His diffidence gone he almost demanded to hold the baby once he'd finished his feed. She placed the child in his father's arms. What a picture they made! How different this all could have been. *You've made your bed, Beth. Oh No! Don't go there.*

Beth and Ryan had lunch together, then went for a walk together, and he was as attentive as any girl could wish. She realised that he was treating her the same way he had treated her parents. It came so naturally to him. He was just an all-round nice guy. But there was a line over which he didn't tread. An essential part of him he held back.

She didn't know it but he was behaving with an unusual amount of circumspection. Once or twice he'd caught a glimpse of something that gave him hope and he wasn't going to mess it up by charging in like a bull. Ryan had decided to woo her. As days go they had a pretty good one. Then Howard walked in.

Beth and Ryan both came out to greet him and Howard almost stepped backwards, but the big Irishman couldn't have been more affable.

'Good to see you, Howard,' he said, shaking his hand warmly. 'Seems our little chap's a fighter, doesn't it? I'm happy to sit here with him a while if you and Beth want to go and get coffee, or a meal.'

Howard eyed him suspiciously, not trusting this change in attitude, but he could detect nothing but openness in the welcome he'd received. Maybe his previous abruptness had been due to worry about his son or jealousy because of what he imagined was the situation between Howard and Beth. He looked to Beth for a lead but she didn't give him any help so he responded in kind.

'I wouldn't mind, if you don't. I've been charged with a couple of things from the office that we need to discuss so it would be a good opportunity.'

'Why don't you both just talk about

me as if I'm not here?' But she was smiling too.

Ryan went back into the unit to hold the baby and felt his insides turn to mush for this little scrap he loved so much. Beth and Howard went off to the coffee shop.

'So Simon's finally realised that he can't run the business without me, has he?'

Howard smiled but brought her straight down out of the clouds. 'Not exactly. That bit was a fib. Actually everything's going on fine — '

'Don't you dare say without me.'

' — without you.' Howard rather thought Beth's was a lot more cheerful now that Ryan was back, and he really wished he knew what was going on there.

'I just wanted you to know. I can't tell anyone else. I'm seeing Jasper tomorrow night; we're going out for dinner.'

'Oh but that's great, Howard, isn't it?'

'The jury's out on that one at the moment. I was so excited when he phoned. He said he thought he'd made a mistake and wanted to come back; and then I thought, what if it happens again in another two or three years? I don't know if I can go through all that again.'

'Do you still love him?'

'Unreservedly.'

'What are you waiting for then?' said Beth, who was of the opinion that she'd give absolutely anything if she were offered another chance. 'Love doesn't come along so often that anyone can afford to cast it aside. Of course you don't want to be hurt again but neither do you want to live your life in loneliness wondering what might have been.' *Like I am*, she thought.

They finished coffee and made their way back. Waving at Ryan through the glass Howard left and Beth went in to join him.

'So tell me, is it all falling apart without you?'

'They're just about getting by.'

There was a comfortable feeling between them that both appreciated, that neither tried to explain and which left them both with a sensation of wellbeing. Ryan was still keeping behind the line though. He was being very careful. It occurred to Beth that if Howard and Jasper did get back together she would be homeless again and that was worrying. As a new mother the last thing she wanted to have to think about was where she and Patrick would live. She was just about to tell Ryan when she realised that he had no idea what the real situation was.

* * *

'Hi, Siobhán, it's Ryan.'

'I was hoping you'd phone. I can get so much more out of you than from a text. How is everything there?'

'It's going really well. Patrick has been out of his incubator now for over thirty-six hours without any apparent complications and he's putting on weight. If he carries on at this rate they've said he can go home in a week or so.'

'That's great news, Ryan. What will you do then? Obviously you can't stay with Beth.'

'Well I'm working on it; my plan that is, not staying with Beth. She seems a bit unsure herself what she's going to do. She's talking about going to her parents for a while.'

'Is that too far from the hotel for you to go and see them?'

'If it is, I'll move hotels.'

'How are you getting on, the two of you?'

Ryan smiled to himself, not really sure but he had a good feeling about it. Problem was Howard was still on the scene. He couldn't say that he'd felt any passion between them so, although under normal circumstances there was no way he'd interfere, in this case his son's future was at stake and he'd rather it was spent with him. Apart from which, in spite of keeping it well hidden from her, there was no doubt in his mind that he wanted to spend the rest of his life with Beth. He was deeply in love and treading very carefully. He couldn't afford to lose her twice.

'We're getting along okay. No huge arguments at least. We'll have to see what happens after next week when Patrick is allowed to leave hospital.'

'Ryan?'

'Yes.'

'Don't you want to know how the business is going?' He could hear the smile in her voice.

'Not in the least. I couldn't have left it in more capable hands. Talk to you in a couple of days. Bye.'

'Bye.'

Ryan thought perhaps it was time to talk to Beth about logistics. He didn't want to push her but he did want to make sure she was comfortable when the time came.

'Have you got enough room in your flat? I know I haven't seen it but I get the impression it's quite small.'

It wasn't that the flat was small, though it was. What really mattered was that Howard and Jasper had had a successful reunion and though he wouldn't rush her, and the two men were sharing a room and wouldn't need the one she was using, it was also obvious and very understandable that they'd prefer to have the place to themselves. Like it or not she was going to have to find somewhere else to live. This would be her third move in less than a year and now she had a baby to worry about as well.

'It's manageable but I'll only go there initially to collect some stuff. Patrick and I are going to stay with my parents.'

'And Howard?' A week ago he wouldn't have dared ask the question but by this time he had serious doubts as to the basis of that particular relationship.

'No, he's going to stay on at the flat. He needs to be able to get to work.' It was a reasonable reply; it could have been true.

'Perhaps I could hire a car then. Take you to collect whatever you need and drive you to your parents.'

The hole she'd dug for herself was getting bigger.

* * *

The day Patrick was due to leave hospital Ryan was still in his hotel room when the phone rang.

'Ryan, it's Siobhán. You are not going to believe this.'

He could hear something in her voice that worried him. He sat on the bed, his pulse rate suddenly accelerated.

'What is it? Mam? Dad?'

'No. Nothing like that. It's good news. They've found him, Ryan. They've got him.'

Ryan went milky white; not easy for a man of his complexion.

'He's admitted it. How could he not? They've got his fingerprints after all. Evidently there's no connection between you at all. You've never even met the man. They picked him up in the commission of a crime — I think that was the expression they used. It was all over for him after that. The Garda asked me if I wanted to give you the news. After all, if they've never charged you they can hardly tell you now that you're off the hook. But you are, Ryan. You are.'

He wasn't quite sure how to handle the news, it had been hanging over him for so long. Like the hangman's noose, hovering just above his head. It took him some time to calm down enough to button his shirt then he spent the short journey in the hire car wondering how he was going to break the news to Beth. This altered everything for him; he could stake his claim without the Sword of Damocles poised above him. What if he'd been wrong in his reading of her? They'd have to take giant steps backwards and build a relationship again based just on their shared parenthood. He decided to wait until he got her back to the flat. The hospital was not the place to have a conversation on which the rest of his life depended — and Beth's and Patrick's.

Beth was waiting with Patrick, pretty excited about leaving the hospital where she felt she been for an eternity; even more terrified of what would happen next. The one thing she was truly grateful for was that it was a weekday and Howard was at work. He had asked her if she wanted him to stay at home but that was a definite no, not if Ryan was driving her to her parents.

Apart from the necessary exchange of information as far as directions were concerned they completed the journey in silence, each with their own agenda, each knowing the rest of their life was in the balance. It took half an hour and by the time they got there Beth was a quivering wreck. She unlocked the door and went in front of him.

'I'll just put Patrick in his cot so I've got a free pair of hands; I won't be a minute.' But he followed her into the minute bedroom, noticing as she opened the small wardrobe that her clothes were hanging there. He began to speak but she put a finger over her lips and gestured to the door. They went into the small sitting room, no remains now of the curry that had been here the last time she been at home.

'It's a very small bedroom.'

'Yes.'

'With a single bed.'

'Yes.'

'Where does Howard sleep?'

'Over there.' She pointed. 'He's gay, Ryan.' So that was what Siobhán meant.

'There's something I have to tell you, Beth.'

'I know; we have to talk about Patrick's future.'

'There's something you need to know first. When I went back to Dublin the week before last it was because of the hearing; about the accident.' Her eyes opened wide. 'They'd found proof of tampering and fingerprints but those prints weren't held on their database.

They only knew that they weren't mine.'

'Why didn't you tell me?'

'Because until they found who they belonged to I could have been an accomplice, even the instigator. There was no proof that I was involved but there was no proof either that I wasn't.'

'And you're telling me now because . . . ?'

'Siobhán phoned just before I left the hotel. They caught him doing another job. There's no connection between us at all. The nightmare is over, Beth.'

She went an even whiter shade of pale than he had earlier. Then red patches crept up and adorned her cheeks. They stared at each other, silence stretching between them until there was a small cry from the bedroom. As one they moved to see their son and as Beth lifted Patrick out of his cot Ryan's gaze fell on a framed photo on the bedside table. They made a handsome couple, he in his dinner jacket towering over her as she held a red rose, the picture taken at the captain's formal dinner on the second night of the cruise. His eyes flew to hers and held them, the hint of a question though by now he knew the answer. Then he looked down at Patrick sleeping peacefully in her arms.

'He's dropped off again. Put him back in the cot, Beth.' The blood raced through his body. If she hadn't been holding the baby he'd have grabbed hold of her.

'But . . . '

'Now, Beth; put him in the cot now.'

Powerless to resist, she did as she was told.

'I think the time has come to stop hiding, don't you?'

Her feelings threatened to overwhelm her so much she almost couldn't stand. Hands on her shoulders he held her away from him, just as he had all those months ago, and looked into her eyes. This time, as then, he was satisfied with what he saw there. He folded his arms around her. At last Beth had found her safe harbour. At long last she had come home.